# SOMEWHERE
## *on*
## GOTLAND ISLAND

# VERNA ELLIOTT HUTLET

This book is a work of fiction. Names, characters, places, and incidents either are products of the author's imagination or are used fictitiously. Any resemblance to actual persons, living or dead, events, or locales is entirely coincidental.

**Somewhere on Gotland Island**

© **2015, Verna Elliott Hutlet**
**ISBN** 978-0-9947439-0-9

Hutlet, Verna Elliott.

Somewhere on Gotland Island / Verna Elliott Hutlet

1. Fiction 2. Mystery

First Edition

10 9 8 7 6 5 4 3 2 1

Dedicated to

MY DAD & MOM

## Wallace & Lena (Preston-Lundgren) Elliott

of Welsh / Dutch-Scotch & Swedish-Norwegian ancestry

**and to my husband, Robert(Herby)**

our six children and their families

**Tammy, Mark, Lauri, Joanne, Jay, Jacalyn**

to my 5 siblings & their families

**Norma, Lillian, Rhondda, Earl, Sandra**

.

and to a dog called Waldo

**Gotland Island** is an actual island off the mainland of Sweden, known as the *"Treasury of the World"*. It was a major trading centre in medieval times and even today, coins from many countries, as well as pirate treasures, are discovered there.

# 1

Cassidy couldn't think of anyone close to her Uncle Raglan other than her father and herself. She never saw him at a coffee shop with friends, and only an odd car stopped in his driveway for a short time before driving away. She thought he would have made an excellent lighthouse keeper, only indulgent to remote ships who kept their distance.

Raglan Leslie lived in a large, three-story house of Victorian architect, which sprawled along the banks of Salter River. Due to ghost stories about the place for the past five years, Cassidy's mother was forever closing the living room curtains so she couldn't view the mansion on the other side of the river, but it never bothered Cassidy to accompany her father for a visit to the enchanting house.

She had always wondered what secrets lie up the unexplored staircase in her uncle's home, but Uncle Raglan solemnly warned that ghosts would toss her off the banister if she climbed any higher than ground level. He spoke with such conviction that she controlled her curiosity to explore further.

When Raglan moved to the Oakside Nursing Home in his eighty-eighth year, the abandoned house was spared the vandalism many old houses succumb to when people think they are unoccupied. Undoubtedly, ghost stories saved her uncle's property and indoor contents from theft. Other than her father's occasional visits to check on the place, the dwelling was pretty much left to solitude, excluding the occasional rumor of lights glowing from the attic.

Cassidy discovered herself heir to the mansion after her uncle died. Her father said it was because she was the only person not intimidated by local ghost stories, and could hand a cup of tea to the man without shaking so much as to spill hot tea over his fingers. The explanation amused Cassidy, as she imagined she was the only person Raglan Leslie ever invited in for tea.

A sagging veranda surrounded two sides of the house, and if you ran your hand down the exterior walls, the peeling paint would crackle and crumble in your palm like sun-dried orange peels. Windows in the high tower appeared cracked, and shingles were missing on the roof peak. The once groomed lawns were now long with grass and weeds, and buried in a three-year blanket of fallen leaves. Cassidy knew it was in her best financial interest to have the old building torn down, and sell the land for new development, especially if no one was to live there, but Cassidy loved history. When her eyes embraced the once-beautiful Victorian architect of the mansion, it seemed a shame to destroy something so historical.

The ground-level rooms in her uncle's mansion were filled with antique furniture, artifacts and old paintings with wide, gold-gilded frames that were more attractive than the stiff portraits they encompassed. Cassidy was especially attracted to a carpet hung on the far wall in the tea room. Her uncle once explained that it was a Chinese carpet, which he himself had brought from the orient as a wedding present for his bride many years before, and that he was pleasantly surprised to see his wife had kept it after their separation.

He informed his niece that designs on Chinese carpets were different from other carpets. Chinese carpets were rarely decorative, but had exact meaning. He pointed to central medallions in the carpet and explained that the characters represented long life, luck and wedded bliss. The autumn chrysanthemum in the pattern was a symbol of longevity and the peony flower, symbolic of nobility, riches and love. When her uncle explained the meanings in the carpet, Cassidy could sense his affection for his wife, and it saddened her to know something had happened to cause their separation years before she was born.

When she questioned her father about his brother's wife, he merely patted her shoulder and said, "Love between a man and woman is like a valentine, bright and beautiful, but it balances on a very tiny point. If your love fades due to lack of attention to each other, the heart can flip upside down, and become a black spade; the symbol of distrust. If the heart tips on its side, it can become an arrowhead, shooting off in either direction, looking for satisfaction somewhere else. Love is like that. You have to nourish love to keep it balanced upright on that tiny point....Let's just say their lifestyles caused them to become arrows." The explanation puzzled Cassidy at the time, but as she grew older, she better understood her father's interpretation of love, and vowed that should she ever meet a man she would marry, she would slip a valentine into his pocket often to remind him of her love.

～～～

As an only child, Cassidy had the overwhelming task of dealing with the contents inside the Salter River Mansion. Her mother was dreadfully scared to walk through the front door for fear of ghosts, and her father was stationed overseas in the army, so neither parent was available to help with decisions. Her only aunt and cousins on her mother's side lived provinces away, so the house and contents were now the sole responsibility of thirty-seven year old, Cassidy Jacalyn Leslie.

Cassidy lived with her mother in a rental apartment building, partly because her father was gone for much of the time on army duties overseas, and partly because her mother needed assistance after obtaining a leg injury in a car accident sixteen years before. It came as a surprise to Cassidy when her mother suddenly announced that she had decided to move into the Hilltop Senior Complex where her friends of similar age lived. Cassidy sensed her mother was doing this to allow her daughter freedom to make her own way in life, but it was difficult for Cassidy to leave her comfort zone.

The young lady now had to make the decision on where she would live. After discussing her finances with an accountant, she realized the taxes and expense of keeping Uncle Raglan's mansion on four acres would eventually eat up the value of the property, so she had no choice but to sell it.

"First things first", Cassidy told herself, and that was to take stock of what lie inside the mansion. To save time and rent somewhere else, she decided to move into her uncle's house, ghost or no ghost, until she could weigh her options. Until she encountered ghosts herself, she refused to believe in the tales of strange lights occasionally glowing from the attic, and the piercing howl of a wolf about the grounds after midnight.

Cassidy put most of her belongings in storage, and arrived at the Salter River mansion with two suitcases in hand. She surveyed the winding staircase and decided there would be time enough for exploring upstairs tomorrow when sunlight brightened the dark corners. For this first night, she chose to sleep on a large sofa close to the front door, just in case something disturbed her and she wanted to make a quick exit.

With shoulders squared and chin up, she whipped the sheets off some of the furniture and chose a table for her computer. She placed her photos on the fireplace mantle, and lit a perfumed candle, which her mother had given her, so that its fresh floral aroma could overpower the lingering scent of Uncle Raglan's cigar smoke and lemon-oiled wood.

~⁓⁓~

*From the attic, a head jerked erect at the sound of intrusion in the lower level of the mansion. A thin man unlocked the attic door and slipped down the steps to the second story level in the house. From there, he entered a closet, whose side wall opened at the pressure of his hand. Like a silent serpent, he slipped down the secret, narrow staircase to the lower level, and leaned his eye close*

*to a peephole, which he had carved through the wall to witness*
*what was going on in the main room of the mansion. He watched*
*Cassidy settle into the house, and the slightest whisper escaped*
*from his lips. "Damn!"*

Cassidy had taken a two month leave of absence from work to allow herself time to dig full force into sorting out belongings in the house and make decisions on selling the property. She wished her father was not overseas and that he could advise her on what paperwork was important to keep, as there seemed to be mountains of files stacked on every shelf and in every cabinet of the room. It puzzled Cassidy because she had never seen such files at any time when she last visited her uncle, and her father had never mentioned them whenever he went to check on the house after his brother moved to the Oakside Nursing Home. The files were carelessly stacked and thrown about, which was not in character with how her uncle would have kept them. Once being an army man, Uncle Raglan's tablecloth was even smoothed without a wrinkle to ice-surface perfection.

Cassidy finally decided to salvage boxes from the local grocery store, and start storing the files in boxes. Then at a later date, when her father returned on leave, they could go through the files together to see what was worth keeping and what wasn't. At least it would clear the shelves off, and make the place appear less cluttered.

After filling thirty-six boxes with dusty files, Cassidy sat down on the sofa for a break. By now, she realized that something was abnormal about the volume of files. Some files contained nothing but confusing financial lists, while others listed company names and phone numbers unfamiliar to her. Nothing seemed to be in any alphabetical or numerical order, not even any yearly order. It was hard to determine whether the files were valuable or a bunch of junk, as none appeared relevant to anything she knew her uncle was involved in. She needed a second opinion and thought of Adam Lucino.

Adam lived in a house beside the rental apartment building where Cassidy previously lived. She would often see him mowing the lawns at the apartment complex, and concluded that he was the caretaker, as he seemed forever dressed in work attire and covered with green, leafy cuttings from trimming hedges and lawns. Adam didn't stand out as being handsome or anything extra-ordinary, so he wasn't the kind of fellow that hit a girl like a bolt of lightning. His shaggy black hair looked like he'd taken his own hedge clipper to it. He had a slightly crooked nose, and walked with a limp from a hockey accident years before. He often teased her mother that if they put their two good legs together, they could probably skate quite well.

She had known Adam for several years. However, they were like two planets traveling on separate orbits. He would merely stop what he was doing and nod, "Good Morning", as she left the apartment for work at the dental office, and she would smile back, thinking it unfair that the poor guy had both a crooked smile and a crooked nose, not to mention a lame leg…and could use a haircut.

Now, as Cassidy sat and tried to think of someone she could trust to invite into her uncle's house and view the valuables without returning with a semi-truck to steal them, the only person who popped into her head was Adam Lucino. He fixed everything in the apartments from plumbing and heating to repairing doors and windows, and she had never heard one complaint from the tenants about his integrity.

# 2

Adam knelt down and rummaged through boxes of papers, a confused frown wrinkling his brow. His large tan-colored dog sat quietly on the floor beside him, one paw over Adam's knee as if to proclaim Adam his private property. Cassidy crouched down beside the young man and waited for his opinion. Adam looked across the sea of boxes spread across the living room rug. "And you say nothing is in yearly order or any order whatsoever?"

"Nothing that I can figure out," Cassidy replied with a shake to her head. She flipped through a handful of papers and dropped them back in the box with a defeated look on her face. "I can't see Uncle Raglan leaving these files when he went to Oakside without first informing someone as to what they were about. The files were not here when I last visited him in this house, and Dad has never mentioned them." Cassidy stood up and sighed in exasperation. "I couldn't get hold of Dad overseas to ask about the files...and Mom has never stepped foot in the place, so she's of no help with anything in here. I don't want to throw anything away if it's valuable, but I also don't want to live in a place that looks like a bomb hit the library."

Adam ran fingers through his disorderly, raven hair. Each box contained at least fifty files and he contemplated that it might take weeks to go through them all thoroughly. "Well," he suggested, "maybe we'll see some kind of pattern forming once we get a few boxes sorted in yearly order."

Cassidy put her hand on his jacket sleeve for one moment. "Are you sure you want to get involved in all this work? It might wind up worthless." Adam's dog rose and whined at seeing her hand touch Adam. She quickly withdrew her hand for fear the dog might bite her.

Adam spoke to the dog, and then smiled at her. "He's not protective. He just doesn't want to share my attention."

Cassidy chuckled with relief, "I imagine that cuts into your lo...." She bit her lip and looked shyly away. She was about to say "love life", and was thankful that it had not spilled from her lips, but Adam picked up on what she meant anyway, and laughed.

"Well now, I never thought of that. Maybe Waldo's the reason the ladies aren't knocking down my door." He used the wooden armrest on the sofa to push himself to his feet. He limped over to a table and dumped out a box of files. "If we find nothing, we'll just have a big bonfire and roast wieners when we're done." He picked up two files, "Where do you want to start organizing these papers?"

Cassidy looked around and saw the rows of empty shelves that she had recently cleared off. "We can start placing the categories by year on the shelves." She turned and stumbled over his dog who had conveniently placed himself between her and Adam like the Great Wall of China.

"He's rather...BIG, isn't he?" She envisioned the dog consuming half of Adam's salary in dog food. She reached out gingerly to pat Waldo's huge head, hoping a peaceful truce might save her from being swallowed whole. The dog wagged his tail and leaned against her leg to receive additional attention.

"He's half St. Bernard." Adam informed her. "I mentioned to my father once that I'd like to get a dog. Before I had chance to consider one, he walked into my house with this monster, and said, "Now THIS is a dog." I think Papa had fearful images of me walking down the street with a less than macho dog, which might cast embarrassment to his Lucino name."

He smiled widely, and Cassidy noticed that his crooked smile concealed white perfect teeth. As a dentist, she noticed such things. Adam continued, "Fortunately, my father owns 40 acres outside the city, so Waldo gets most of his exercise out there chasing Merlin…the family cat."

Waldo followed Cassidy around the room like a persistent shadow, and she didn't know how to escape him. She kept patting the dog's head, hoping his desire for affection would eventually be satisfied, but Waldo was completely addicted to his newfound source. Finally, Adam took mercy on Cassidy and signaled the dog to his side. "Time out, Waldo!" Then he turned to her with humor, "You know Waldo feels he's doing you a favor by letting you pat him."

Cassidy smiled back and relaxed in Adam's wit. She had been stressed since the death of her uncle, trying to deal with legal matters and now the ambush of mysterious files. "Perhaps I should borrow him as a guard dog," she replied. "No ghost would dare to cross a dog that size."

Adam blew dust off a file and asked, "Do you believe in the ghost stories about this place?...You know, I have seen lights in the attic a few times when taking late night walks with Waldo. Likely just your uncle looking for something. Thought I heard a wolf howl once, but it could have been a coyote or dog. Hard to tell from across the river. Waldo here, gave a howl back, but no wolf replied." He affectionately ruffled his dog's ears. "Waldo was actually relieved not to get an answer, weren't you, boy?"

Cassidy sighed and plunked herself down on the sofa. "Enough stories about lights in attics and wolf howls. It's taking all the guts I have to sleep here until I get things in order."

Adam's brown eyes softened in sympathy. "Sorry! Anyhow, I'll stay tonight and keep working on these files, if you like. That should keep the ghosts away for at least tonight. You got a coffee pot?" She nodded and turned towards the cupboard in hopes that her uncle had stored coffee somewhere.

Cassidy removed the lid of the coffee pot and pulled out an unexpected piece of paper. She eyed the list of three unfamiliar phone numbers and then handed it to Adam. "I don't recognize any of these phone numbers, but Uncle must have hidden the list in the coffee pot for either Dad or myself. I doubt if anyone else would be using the coffee pot."

Adam scanned his eyes down the list of foreign phone numbers. "How about if I call one of the numbers on this list and ask about their association with your uncle. Maybe a simple answer will clear this mystery up, and we won't have to go through all these boxes. He might have been simply storing files for some company."

Cassidy shook her head negatively as she handed him her cell phone. "Doesn't sound like something my uncle would do. He liked his privacy, and wouldn't take to people tramping in here to dump off files all the time...and he was an army man...neat as feathers on a Mallard duck. He wouldn't allow a mess like this...and once he was in the Oakside Nursing Home, he certainly wouldn't have strangers coming in and out of the mansion with all the antiques in this place. Something isn't right." She turned back to the cupboard to make coffee while Adam chose a number at random from the list.

A voice on the other end of the phone answered abruptly, "Your time was up eight months ago. It's a little late to bargain now."

The voice sounded very agitated, so Adam kept his voice low and conversation short. He suspected the receiver thought he was speaking to Cassidy's uncle. "Never too late to bargain," Adam uttered, hoping to calm the upset voice on the other end of the line.

A threatening voice fired back, "You ready to make up the twenty million the boss lost from waiting for that Harja file or are you ready to deliver it?...If not, they'll find you floating in Lake Superior along with Simco. Maybe you'll run across him." A wicked laugh filled the phone.

Adam pressed "Off" on the phone with lightning speed. Horror crossed his face as he glanced quickly at Cassidy. "Sakes alive, girl! What was your uncle involved in? I think I just got a death threat."

Cassidy sat on the edge of the sofa, rocking back and forth with her arms wrapped about her torso like a protective cocoon. Waldo plunked his huge head down upon her lap, but Cassidy was too upset to acknowledge the dog's goodwill efforts. "Oh no," Cassidy kept repeating in fear. "What have I inherited? I thought all I had to contend with were ghost stories and taxes eating up the place."

# 3

Adam tried to calm Cassidy, and shoved a mug of freshly-made coffee into her hands. "Here, take a sip of coffee, and breathe slowly." She grabbed the cup with both trembling hands and inhaled the deep coffee aroma. Her mind was whirling, trying to think of what her uncle could possibly be involved in to cause something as violent as death threats. She barely knew her uncle, other than having casual visits where she listened in on her father and uncle's old army tales. Her uncle could be capable of anything and she would never suspect it.

"Do you know anyone called Simco?" Adam asked, and Cassidy shook her head negatively. Just two, frightened blue eyes peered at Adam above the rim of her coffee cup. "Maybe I misunderstood," Adam contemplated, "but he did say your uncle owed him twenty million dollars or some file, or..." His hand made the sinister gesture of slitting his throat.

Cassidy silently mouthed the figures back to him, "Twenty...million...dollars?"

Adam nodded the affirmative. He hated to frighten her, but there was no sense hiding the truth. He stared at the list of numbers. "They asked for a Harja file. Does that sound familiar to you?"

Cassidy shook her head, and continued to bury her nose

even deeper in the coffee cup so he wouldn't notice tears dampening the corner of her eyes.

Adam scanned the boxes again. "It'll be in here somewhere. I have a feeling this was your uncle's way of hiding the file in case they came looking for it. Where better to hide a diamond than in a sea of diamonds."

"Maybe we should burn it all," Cassidy suggested with a defeated attitude. "Then they'd leave us...me...alone...or tell them the truth that my uncle died and I have no idea what they're talking about...and they can look for it themselves."

"I highly doubt they'll believe you if the file is worth twenty million dollars. They'll think you kept it to blackmail them with, or sell to someone else. Sorry! But they are not going to rest until they have it...or our heads."

"I'm so sorry for involving you in this," Cassidy cried, looking sadly about the room adorned with antique furniture. "I thought this was going to be like a treasure hunt, unveiling beautiful artifacts and hidden history. I was so looking forward to it. Maybe we should call the police."

Adam strongly disagreed. "We really have no proof of anything to report. Just a phone call. These people, whoever they are, will deny they threatened me. They'll say I misunderstood on the phone, and then they'll find out who you are, where you live, where your mother lives...the whole bit." He looked at the list of names again. "Best we find that Harja file fast, but I'm not quite sure what to look for." He looked her straight in the eye. "Looks like your family didn't know your uncle very well."

Cassidy tried desperately to remember some past conversation, which might reveal a clue as to what her uncle was involved in, but she could think of nothing. "Both Uncle and my Dad served in the army for many years," Cassidy revealed to Adam. "Uncle always seemed very patriotic and honorable to me, but one never knows. People can have secrets."

She sat the coffee cup down and walked over to a Roman pillar stand near the base of the long, winding staircase. Her fingers traced over the smooth, white curves of a marble horse statue perched upon the pillar stand. "I can't believe Uncle Raglan would deliberately leave me trouble. I'm sure he would only want to leave me beautiful things."

"I don't like to rain on your parade, Miss, but he must have known he owed someone a valuable file or he wouldn't have tried to hide it in all this mess. Surely he expected someone to come collecting after he passed away."

Cassidy sniffed up a runny nose, trying not to tear up again. She didn't want to look frightened, but fear was squeezing her chest like a vice. This was no movie or fairytale. She wandered aimlessly about the spacious living room, looking up at magnificent old paintings of people she wasn't even related to. "Uncle only lived in this house for about eight years. All this splendid furniture, paintings and fixtures came with the house from his wife. I don't think Uncle Raglan uncovered half the sheets over it. He stuck to living in a couple rooms on this ground level. He said his eighty year old legs couldn't take to climbing stairs...and kidded that a ghost would toss anyone over the balcony if they tried."

"He was married?"

"For about three years, then separated. No kids. I never met his wife. My father and Uncle Raglan were both born in Wales, and Uncle Raglan met her there. They separated before I was born. About fifty years later, Uncle Raglan found out she had died and left him this property in her will. Uncle used to say she likely gave him the place because it was haunted and hoped the ghosts would get him...but I like to think a love connection was there somewhere."

"Or a crime. Maybe his wife's family was into something, and your uncle inherited the problem with the house...like you have. Strange that his wife's property just happened to be across the river from where your father lived."

Cassidy agreed that the coincidence was unusual. "Uncle Raglan was in the army for most of his life, and never seemed to have a home of his own that I remember. I thought maybe his wife purchased this property so Uncle could live his later years close to my father...but maybe that wasn't the reason." She opened her laptop computer. "Harja! Maybe it's a company name. Let's see what we can find out on the computer."

Cassidy read aloud: *The Vimose Comb, an ancient comb from around AD150, was discovered in a bog on the island of Funen, Vimose, Denmark. The Vimose Comb has the oldest known runic inscription, a simple male's name of HARJA inscribed on the comb.*

"Runes," Adam exploded with excitement. "I loved ancient history in school. I believe runes were originally magic signs for charms, and that rune means secret or something hidden." Adam's face was suddenly very close to hers, looking intently at the computer screen. "Runes were first derived from an alphabet used among Italic tribes, and evolved into language groups by different cultures around the 2nd or 3rd century."

Cassidy turned her face to look at him with raised eyebrows, surprised and impressed at his historic knowledge on runes.

Adam laughed at the shocked expression on her face. "So you thought all I knew was how to cut grass?"

Cassidy's cheeks flushed with embarrassment. "Of course not. I thought...I thought...you were a very good...caretaker."

"Maybe," he smiled in amusement at her embarrassment, and then gave a little wink. "But I was better as a hockey player."

Cassidy knew his knee had been injured playing hockey, and her face saddened at the loss of his hockey career.

Adam reassured her with a crooked grin, "Don't worry. If I'd stayed in hockey, I'd likely have wound up with a broken nose or leg...Come to think of it, I DID wind up with a broken nose and leg." He shrugged his shoulders in a nonchalant manner. "Guess I should have been a bull rider."

Adam pressed his face close to the computer screen again. "We could be looking for something ancient, inscribed with rune characters." There was fresh excitement in Adam's voice, but Cassidy was not quite so enthusiastic. The death threat weighed heavy on her shoulders.

Cassidy took her eyes off the computer screen and once

again, surveyed the contents of the large room about them. "I can't imagine Uncle Raglan having anything to do with ancient runes. He never even bothered to uncover half the antiques in this house, so why would he be interested in runes?"

She turned her attention back to the computer screen again. "The information on here says runic inscriptions have been found all over Western Europe, especially in England and Scandinavia on stone monuments, metal spear-points and amulets. Uncle Raglan did travel across Europe a lot...and I suppose museum treasures would be tempting to a thief...if Uncle Raglan was a thief."

"Well, there's two more numbers on this list...unless they hang up before I find out anything," Adam said pensively, as he put on his jacket. "Perhaps we'll call from a pay-phone in Kenora this time, just to be on the safe side. People like that can trace you anywhere. We'll use a pay phone."

Cassidy shut down her computer. "And remember, Harja could simply be a name for something else. The file might have nothing to do with runes at all."

The young couple and Waldo stepped out onto the weathered front veranda where pillars revealed natural wood between remnants of peeling, white paint. A thick growth of ivy and honeysuckle vines wound their way up the pillars and onto the veranda roof, as if trying to hide evidence of aging shingles beneath.

Cassidy shivered. "Feels like rain," she said, looking skyward. The moon peeked between clouds, casting long shadows of trees across the lawn like dark, grasping fingers. She felt uneasy, as if someone was watching her from the shadows.

Suddenly, a fearful wolf howl from the nearby woodlot chilled the air, and Waldo turned tail and began scratching at the door to get back inside the house. Cassidy's eyes grew huge with fear and she froze in her tracks, expecting fangs to leap at her throat and drag her to the ground at any moment.

Adam straightened his body and looked about the yard suspiciously. "Keep walking slowly and steadily to my jeep," he instructed, and bent down to take Waldo by the collar in case the dog should rush off into the bush to approach the animal. Waldo, however, had no intentions of such bravery.

The threesome quickly climbed into the jeep and locked the doors with desperate speed. Waldo lowered his head on the back seat of the jeep, as he wanted no part in looking out the window.

"I...I've never heard a howl that close before," Cassidy stuttered through chattering teeth, her nails digging deep into Adam's arm for support. "Weren't you frightened?" She noted Adam had acted very calmly to the situation.

Adam thought to sound heroic, but decided Cassidy would see clear through such fallacy, seeing as his fingers were fumbling to get the key in the ignition. "I near to bit my tongue half off when that thing howled."

Cassidy laughed out loud at his sincerity, as she knew many young men would not admit to such fear, especially in front of a woman. Adam was surely an honest man.

Adam scanned the shaded perimeter of the woodlot beside the house, trying to catch sight of any movement that might be an animal. "Makes no sense that a wolf would be in city limits," he informed her. "Wolf habitat is much farther north in timberland. It's possible that a coyote might have followed rabbits into the city...but not a wolf."

Cassidy had suffered all the drama she needed for one day. She closed her eyes and leaned her head back on the seat, relieved not to be dealing with this crisis alone. Adam slipped his arms out of his jacket, and spread it over her. "Here, use my jacket as a blanket and try to rest while we drive to Kenora. It'll take about an hour to get there. Just think about what the Harja file could be. Don't think about the wolf. We'll take care of him later."

"Thank you!" she whispered with a grateful voice that was depleted of energy. "If you hadn't been here, that wolf howl would have sent me swimming halfway across Salter River by now."

He gazed down into her blue eyes for a few minutes, aware of the rise and fall of her chest breathing beneath his hand on the jacket. He blurted out almost angrily, "Where's your husband...your boyfriend...any friend...to help you in all of this?"

He was observant of all the comings and goings in the apartment complex, and it puzzled him that she always appeared alone, for he considered her a very pleasant and attractive young lady. He felt she should have had someone she could call for help.

26

She should not have needed to call him. They barely knew each other.

"Things just got in the way of friendships," Cassidy confessed somewhat sadly. "Most of my old school chums are married now and moved away. Dad is in the army and gone a lot, so Mom needed me after her accident...Had a boyfriend once, but didn't work out...Then there was University and studying...then my job...just things."

Adam nodded, but did not reply. He understood more than she realized, for the years had flown by for him too, and things simply got in the way of the life and relationships he originally planned for himself.

Cassidy rested her head against the back of the seat in the jeep, his jacket warm upon her as if his body was still in it. She was ever so grateful that she could feel the protective strength of his arm next to hers. She decided his shaggy black hair, and his crooked nose and smile could be viewed as somewhat charming once you knew him. Adam Lucino was like Waldo; a lovable mutt who could worm his way into your heart before you knew it, if you weren't careful.

Then Cassidy silently scolded herself for remotely thinking he was charming. After all, she had fantasies about her special guy someday, and this caretaker covered in leaf cuttings with a crooked nose and smile, and a bum leg certainly wasn't part of the dream.

# 4

Adam pulled into Kenora around ten o'clock in the evening and stopped at a pay phone to call one of the numbers on the list. He clipped a chain onto Waldo's collar, and Cassidy took the dog for a walk while he dug the phone list out of his pocket.

The first number had issued a warning, so he chose to handle the second number on the list very carefully. "About time," the voice threatened without hesitation. "Ulf isn't happy, and when Ulf isn't happy, heads roll...if you get my drift."

Adam breathed in deeply, hoping he would say the right thing. He needed to find out what the file looked like, but had to be careful not to upset the speaker into hanging up the phone before he extracted some clues from him. Adam spoke as forcefully as he dared, trying not to sound easily manipulated.

"You have a new dealer now," Adam stated strongly. "Raglan died before he could tell me where he put the Harja file. I need time to find it."

"You lie."

"No benefit in lying. Check for yourself at the Oakside Nursing Home...Where would he hide the file?"

"Who am I speaking to?"

"Monte...his nephew," Adam quickly lied. He began to panic, for the more he talked, the more lies he had to invent. Adam was not sure he sounded convincing anymore. Lying is like rolling downhill. It's very difficult to back up once you start rolling. The truth is easy to remember, but eventually, it becomes impossible to remember lies. Sooner or later, you dig yourself into a hole.

"Your problem, Monte. If you've picked up his torch, then you've picked up his debt. You've got five days." The phone went dead, and Adam swallowed hard, knowing Cassidy Leslie and himself were slowly being sucked into a situation that might cost them their lives. There was one phone number left on the list, so Adam thought he might as well exhaust all possibilities in finding out what the Harja file looked like. He dialed the number. As he did so, rain started to drip on his shoulders and blur the numbers on the paper.

"You've got nerve making Ulf wait," the voice on the other end of the phone snarled with a definite foreign accent, and Adam gripped the phone tighter. This was his last chance to obtain information. He took a few seconds to control his voice before speaking. He hoped to keep the speaker on the phone long enough to pick up the slightest clue.

This time, Adam decided to try being bluntly honest. "Raglan is dead and hid the file. I don't know what I'm looking for."

Without hesitation, the other voice snapped, "I'd say you're looking for a boat ride five miles from shore. Twenty million or the map deposited in Box 6412, 550 Thor Street in Stockholm as previously arranged. Five days." The phone hung up, and Adam sat down on the curb to wait for Cassidy and Waldo's return. He sheltered the paper from the rain, and quickly wrote down the address, so he wouldn't forget it.

Cassidy returned with Waldo, and could see Adam's solemn face in the street lamp light. She sensed immediately that his news was not going to be good.

Adam glanced up quickly as she approached, raindrops bouncing off his nose and flattening his spiked hair. He did not try to put on a positive air, but looked directly into her face with honesty. His voice was slightly hoarse. "Reached the last two numbers. Got an address where we are to deliver the file but that's about all...Let's get out of this rain. I think I need a strong cup of coffee."

The couple sat across from each other in a small empty restaurant, as rain dribbled down the window pane beside them. "We've got no choice but to look for the file until we tear every board out of the place," Adam gravely informed her. "I hate to say it, but we're in a heap of trouble. They gave us five days to deposit the file in a box in Stockholm."

Cassidy's eyebrows arched and she stuttered, "S...Stockholm? You mean Stockholm, Sweden?" She closed her eyes for a few moments, trying to find an inner calm. "Look! They have no idea who you are. I appreciate you trying to help, but it's not your problem. I'll...just...burn the house down."

Adam leaned forward and peered into her eyes with intensity. "You have a pretty head. I don't want to see it floating in the Great Lakes. Burning the house isn't going to stop them. They believe we have this file... and besides, if you think you're going to take part in an adventure with runes and all that historical stuff without me, well, think again." Adam stood up and beckoned her to follow him to his jeep, where Waldo waited patiently for the hamburger patty he knew Adam would not forget to bring him from the restaurant.

⁓

By three o'clock in the morning, both young people were exhausted from searching, and plunked themselves down on the sofa in defeat. Waldo was stretched out sleeping on half the sofa, so Cassidy used him as a pillow for her head. "What did they exactly say?" she questioned, her voice partly slurred and eyes droopy from want of sleep.

"Just to deposit the map or twenty million dollars in Box 6412 at..." Adam stopped his speech mid-sentence, and frowned. "Did I just say map? Did HE say map? I can't remember. Map! Map! Maybe we should be looking for a map." He jumped up and turned around several times. "Did you come across anything that resembled a map?"

Cassidy was startled out of her sleepy state, and sat up abruptly. "No! Nothing like a map... but we still have lots of boxes to go through." She grabbed a box and started rummaging through the files with fresh adrenalin, looking for a map.

"Stop!" Adam ordered, and she froze at what she was doing. "It's not here," he declared. "These files are decoys. Your uncle wouldn't hide the map where someone could eventually find it. He looked about the room and his eyes drifted to the staircase. "Have you checked upstairs?"

Cassidy shook her head. "I've been tempted, but with all the ghost stories, I was afraid I'd faint into a puddle if so much as a moth touched my shoulder. Besides, Uncle Raglan could never climb those stairs with his poor legs, so I don't think he'd hide a file up there. I doubt if the top floors have been visited since he came here."

"Well, it's time to do some exploring." Adam walked to the base of the wide, winding staircase. "Coming?"

Cassidy rustled in her suitcase and handed him a flashlight. For herself, she removed a large candle from beside the fireplace. "No electricity upstairs that I know of," she informed him. "Uncle only installed electricity downstairs when he came." She unwillingly followed Adam up the staircase into the shadows. "This exploration would have been far less spooky in daylight."

"No time to waste," Adam answered, shining his flashlight up the mysterious dark path before them. "They gave us five days. That's all."

The stairway opened into a long corridor on each side. The left side held four spacious bedrooms, each with tall, floor-length windows, which had invited the sun in for many years and faded the once-bright wallpaper. French-style doors in each bedroom opened onto a long outdoor balcony, shared by the other bedrooms. A stone fireplace in each bedroom shared a chimney with the fireplace in the adjacent bedroom, and accounted for several chimneys protruding from the roof top.

Adam and Cassidy inspected one bedroom at a time, searching for anything that might resemble a map, but the bedrooms held only iron-wrought bed frames without mattresses, simple basin stands and empty dressers with drawers that were dry and difficult to pull out. Some of the bedroom walls displayed large oval frames with curved glass, which made their dreamy country scenes appear three dimensional...but no sign of a map.

After examining the four bedrooms to the left, Adam proceeded down the corridor to the right of the staircase, while Cassidy examined a very large room directly across from the staircase. A semi-circle of windows bowed out at the far end of the room to create a perfect setting for the center of interest, which Cassidy assumed had once been a grand piano, or an orchestra.

About thirty elegant oak chairs with royal blue, velvet-padded seats and intricate carved backrests were piled against one long wall beneath a large tapestry mural. The tapestry covered the full length of the wall, and depicted a Victorian scene where ladies in flowing gowns, danced with gentlemen in a rose garden beside the sea. Cassidy felt a part of the scene, and could sense the music of long ago rebounding from the tapestry. She sat her candle down in the middle of the music room. As if in a trance, Cassidy twirled about in the pretense of dance, her flowing skirt sailing outward like petals on a flower. Having once taken ballet as a teenager, a bygone talent blossomed in her steps once again.

Adam returned from searching elsewhere and paused in the doorway to witness Cassidy twirling in the candlelight. The candle created a round, glowing halo on the hardwood floor and held Cassidy in its light like a centered, fluttering butterfly. Her spinning cast twirling shadows about the walls, and he was spell-bound by the beauty of the effect.

Suddenly, Cassidy noticed him leaning against the door frame, quietly watching her. She bent down quickly and picked up her candle from the floor. It's flame highlighted Cassidy's face like an angel in the dark. "Sorry! I hope I didn't offend the ghosts."

"Not even a ghost would blow out your candle to end such a beautiful sight," Adam said with a gentle, crooked smile that made her knees feel strangely weak for a moment. Then he was gone as quick as the spark of a firefly.

⁓ ⁓ ⁓

"Come see this," Adam called from farther down the hallway.

She followed Adam's voice into a circular tower whose view circled the moonlit grounds below. She looked over the Salter River, flowing in front of the mansion with colorful reflections of city lights from the far shore. "Oh my," she exclaimed in delight. "What a beautiful view. I could get used to living in this house."

"One more flight to climb to the attic in the peak of the house," he informed her, curiosity feeding his spirit, but not hers. He was eager to explore, not minding the dark corners and unexpected discoveries, but Cassidy hesitated to enter the attic, all too aware of ghost stories about a light seen occasionally glowing from the attic window. She reluctantly followed Adam up the narrow staircase.

They discovered the door to the attic locked with a strong bolt and chain, so were unable to gain entrance. Disappointed, Adam descended to the second floor again, while Cassidy felt secretly relieved not to come face to face with a ghost.

"Too bad we couldn't peek in the window," Cassidy sighed, although she was relieved that they were unable to do so.

Adam thought for a few minutes. "Maybe I can. The bedrooms have a balcony outside." She followed him into the first bedroom, and stood back while he opened a door onto the outside balcony. It was raining slightly, so Cassidy remained inside while Adam shone his flashlight up and down the side of the building. "There's a sort of fire escape ladder that runs from ground level up to the roof top," he yelled to her. "I think I can climb the ladder and swing up onto the roof that passes beneath the attic window. If I slip, I'd probably just roll down onto the balcony...or drop onto the veranda overhang...or somewhere in between."

"You're crazy! It's raining and too slippery out," Cassidy argued strongly, sticking her head into the rain just long enough to see his shoes disappear up the ladder into the darkness. "You'll kill yourself," she yelled, but it was too late to stop Adam. Cassidy only knew his whereabouts by the occasional flicker of his flashlight, and the sound of boots scraping on the shingles above. If there was ever a chance for a ghost to cast Adam off the building, now was the ideal time.

The roof was slippery from the rain and occasionally

Adam's shoes slid on the moss-covered shingles, so he lowered himself to crawl on all four knees until he was beneath the attic window. He wiped the rain out of his eyes with his shirt sleeve, being careful not to drop the flashlight in his other hand. He rose carefully to his feet and gripped the window sill with one hand for stability, so that he could shine the flashlight through the open curtain.

It seemed like hours before Cassidy saw his twinkling flashlight return down the ladder. She grabbed a fistful of his wet shirt, and fairly dragged him inside the bedroom door. "Don't do that again. I thought my heart would jump out of my chest, waiting to hear your body rolling off the roof like an acorn."

"Not good news," Adam panted, wiping the rain off his face with the front of his shirt. "I shone my flashlight through the window and from what I can see, someone is living there. We're lucky he wasn't home tonight. The attic looks well lived in with a bed and table, microwave oven, food cans on a shelf, even a small refrigerator and television, which means electricity has been connected up there."

Cassidy put her hand over her mouth in shock. Knots formed in her stomach at the thought of a stranger secretly living in the building, and possibly spying on her and her uncle.

"Surely your uncle must have heard something rustling around up here," Adam expressed with a pinch of frustration. "And hasn't your father ever checked the attic for him?" He pulled the door to the balcony shut and locked it.

"Uncle Raglan was eighty and pretty poor of hearing by the time he came to live here," Cassidy explained, as she followed

Adam down the staircase. "If he did hear anything, he'd likely surmise it was the wind or a mouse. He was so unwavering about no one going upstairs. We just humored him. It was HIS house. I doubt if he'd even hear the wolf howl."

She glanced back up the staircase. "It's also quite possible that this person moved in here after Uncle Raglan went to Oakside. Maybe they thought to take advantage of the vacancy. At least we've solved the mystery of lights in the attic. My ghost appears to have been living quite comfortable...rent-free, I might add."

"I've seen lights occasionally glowing from your uncle's attic window for around five years," Adam informed her. "So that is approximately two or three years before your uncle went to Oakside. Someone took great lengths to hook up electricity and bring in appliances without your uncle's knowledge. Could be the wolf howl was also put on a speaker in the yard to keep people away from discovering his hideout. Whoever is living up there is desperate to stay hidden, which means he could be dangerous. We'd better leave him be for now."

"Did you see a map on the wall or table or anything?" Cassidy asked, quickly remembering that finding the map was the most crucial quest at the moment.

"Nope! All I saw was more trouble to heap on what we've already got."

# 5

Once they were back on the ground floor, Adam advised Cassidy, "You shouldn't stay here alone with a stranger in the attic. I can find you a room at my place, if you wish. We have no time to deal with the attic problem now. First on the list is finding the Harja file."

"Do you think the person in the attic might have something to do with it?" Cassidy asked, suspicious of someone who would go to such great lengths to secretly create a home in the attic of someone else's house. "It's possible he might be looking for the map too. By the looks of these papers tossed about the place, maybe he's the one who has been going through these files looking for it, because I know Uncle Raglan would never leave such a mess."

Droplets of water dripped onto the floor as Adam ran his hand through rain-drenched hair. Cassidy grabbed a towel, threw it over his head and gave it a quick ruffle. When she withdrew the towel, he was standing very close to her, his hair spiked in a million different directions from her towel rub. She stepped back quickly, and figured he was probably born with a wild head of hair that even shocked his mother when she saw him at birth.

As Adam pulled his wet T-shirt off over his head, Cassidy became very aware of his athletic fitness, and shyly turned away so he did not notice how good she thought he looked without a shirt on. She noticed an armband of crossed hockey sticks tattooed around his one bicep, and thought it unfair that he should lose something so dear to his heart.

"Do you have a large sweatshirt or anything dry?" he asked, and she was glad to turn her attention to her suitcase and toss him a hooded shirt with "*I love cats*" on the front. "Aaah, Waldo's not going to like this," Adam complained, as he pulled on the sweat shirt.

Cassidy yawned and sauntered over to the stove, dragging her feet slowly from lack of sleep. "I'll make us a cup of tea to help keep us awake. She carried a teapot and cups into the small tea room. "Let's have a cup of tea in here for old times' sake. I loved sitting in this room with Uncle Raglan. We would sip tea while he explained the significance of every motif on this beautiful old Chinese carpet on the wall. It was a wedding gift for his wife."

As Cassidy and Adam sat at the circular antique table in the tea room to enjoy their tea, Cassidy interpreted the meaningful carpet to Adam. Suddenly, she frowned and rose from her chair to take a closer look at a motif stitched on the corner of the carpet. A small, red rose was stitched over top of the pattern, not noticeable to anyone who wouldn't understand that a rose did not belong in the pattern. She ran her finger over it, and could feel something beneath the stitching.

"What's wrong?" Adam asked, and joined her at the carpet.

"This rose doesn't belong on here," she frowned, her eyes narrowing to view the flower more clearly. "Someone has stitched it onto the carpet...and it feels like something is underneath it. Do you have a knife to snip the threads? Be careful not to harm the carpet underneath."

Adam withdrew a sharp pocket knife and carefully snipped the rose motif stitching. A tiny computer memory card dropped into his palm.

They both looked at each other, eyes wide with surprise and excitement at the discovery. They practically tripped over each other as they raced to the computer to insert the memory card. A message appeared on the computer screen; *"Go to Visby. Find Mikkel."*

"Where the heck is Visby?" Cassidy asked.

"There are two maps on here. One is a general map of Gotland Island, showing Visby as the capital city," Adam revealed with fresh enthusiasm. "The second map is a bit confusing with symbols between places along the coast...like a treasure map."

Cassidy's face leaned in close beside Adam's, her eyes carefully scanning the mysterious map. "I thought the file might show the blueprint of a museum or something, but this seems entirely different. Where's Gotland Island?"

"It's part of Sweden, situated in the Baltic Sea off the mainland. Did your uncle ever mention going there?"

Cassidy's face fell, discouraged that nothing seemed to explain what trouble her uncle was involved in. "I only remember him saying once that he spent his honeymoon in the Baltic Sea."

"Aaah! So maybe there is a connection between your uncle

and Gotland Island."

Adam studied the computer screen once again. "I don't think we should print this map out, or walk around with the small, memory card in our possession. Too easy to lose, or for them to take and toss us in the ocean." He rubbed his chin thoughtfully. "We'll study this map until it is embedded in our minds like a stamp. Then we'll hide the twenty million dollar memory card. That way, we will be too valuable for anyone to destroy."

"I hate to tell you this," Cassidy confessed timidly, "but I'd likely spill everything I know on this map if they started torturing me."

"Good!" Adam praised with a positive pat on her shoulder. "Then you realize you must run very fast."

Cassidy sighed deeply and then sat down at the computer to study the map. "I was hoping Uncle Raglan had no part in this, but only he would know that I would notice a rose didn't belong on the Chinese carpet."

Adam took his turn studying the map. "Well, whatever your uncle was messed up in, he must have entrusted the Harja file to you for a reason...but I sure wish he'd left you with more clues."

"Maybe he kept the clues to a minimum in case the wrong person found the memory card...like my ghost in the attic," Cassidy said in defense of her uncle, and Adam nodded his head in agreement.

Cassidy felt a heavy load weighing her down. "It terrifies me to think that a stranger has been living in the attic, possibly looking for this file for years. He might have snooped around the house while my uncle slept...maybe even watched me from some dark corner in the house. Creepy!" She started grabbing photos off the mantle and throwing them into her suitcase.

Suddenly she paused in her packing. "Yet, when you think of it, the person in the attic hasn't hurt anyone, and if he's been here for around five years, he could have cleaned out the artifacts in this house, and hasn't...so he doesn't appear to be a thief...unless you consider living secretly in someone's house rent-free as theft."

"Maybe he has rich taste," Adam answered wryly. "Why settle for artifacts worth thousands when you can have one worth twenty million? If he robbed articles from this house, his hide-out would soon be discovered, and his chance of finding the Harja file gone...It's a possibility that he's just some homeless person who found a vacant spot to live in, like a country mouse in a shoe, but I highly doubt it. I believe there is some connection between him and this file, but we have no time to deal with him now."

Cassidy stepped into Adam's jeep, and reached an arm back to pat Waldo. "They'll suspect we have the file by now," she mumbled half to herself, calculating the hours and days that made up the five day time frame given to deliver the file.

"Yes, but they won't know Waldo has it." Adam informed her. "We'll find this Mikkel, but I'm not handing any information over to him or anyone else until I know we are free and safe from involvement in this mess forever. I don't want anyone coming back in a few years to blackmail or threaten us ever again." He looked in the back seat at Waldo. "I'll hide the chip in Waldo's collar. Waldo can stay on my father's acreage until we get back. We've got the file in our brain and that's the safest place for it right now, because no one is going to destroy us if we are the file itself."

Cassidy wasn't too sure of that.

# 6

Cassidy was half asleep as she entered Adam's house, and followed him to a bedroom door in the hallway. "Tell the landlord, I'll pay him when I get back from my trip," she muffled, as she tried to suppress a yawn.

"You're my guest," he replied, "No charge."

Cassidy argued with tired, sagging shoulders. "I always pay my way. Then I don't owe any favors." She yawned again and sank against the bedroom door.

Adam looked into her sleepy eyes, reached his arm around her back and turned the bedroom door knob. She stumbled backwards into the room and he closed the door gently between them. "Good night! See you in the morning at six o'clock. We have to take Waldo out to my parents before we catch the plane."

Cassidy awakened to poached eggs, toast and a fruit salad, graciously prepared by her host. As no other guests appeared for breakfast, she asked, "Do you rent this whole house?"

"Sort of. I think Waldo has scared the rest of them off." Adam hurried down the hallway to his own bedroom and returned with a couple backpacks. "You can put some of your stuff into one for traveling. I phoned last night and have tickets booked to the international airport in Arlanda, near Stockholm.

From there, we'll get transportation to Visby on Gotland Island. You can pay me later...seeing as you don't want to owe me any favors."

Cassidy's face flushed, and she was glad she had a piece of toast shoved in her mouth so she couldn't reply. She knew it would take a trillion favors to pay Adam back for what he was doing for her.

"Best we get on the road," Adam advised. "I'm dropping Waldo off at my parents. Father is driving us to the airport. Oh, and I should warn you that my parents are Italian and they will probably have us married by the time we reach the airport."

Cassidy's eyes snapped open while Adam calmly unplugged the coffee pot and toaster, as if his announcement was simply forecasting the weather for the day. "Unless I have six hours to explain our situation to Mama, she will be convinced we are eloping and that would break her heart because she imagines this big wedding with a million relatives kissing my cheek....So by the time we drive to the airport, she'll have something planned."

Cassidy laughed, as she transferred some belongings into the smaller backpack. "I hope you're kidding."

Adam didn't take back his statement. "You've been warned," he said. He turned in the doorway to lock the door just as a breeze caught hold of Cassidy's pastel pink skirt, and fluttered it in the wind. "I'm glad you wore something nice...for our wedding photos."

Cassidy shook her head at Adam, and followed him to his jeep. Waldo jumped into the backseat, unaware that inserted and stitched between two layers of leather on his collar, was a twenty million dollar memory chip. Last night as Cassidy slept, Adam had concealed the Harja file in a waterproof encasement and carefully stitched it into the dog's collar.

Shortly before they arrived at the Lucino residence, Adam stopped the car on the side of the road, took her hand, and slid a ring onto her finger. "This will save a lot of questions. Just tell Mama it's your engagement ring."

Cassidy protested and went to remove the ring.

Adam pulled once again into the traffic and continued to drive. "Suit yourself, but if Mama thinks we're going off on a trip together without so much as an engagement ring, she'll probably contact the pilot to marry us on the plane...I think pilots can do that...like a ship captain...can't they?"

"Oh for Pete's sake!" Cassidy exclaimed with frustration and slipped the ring back on her finger. "Where did you get this little thing...out of a popcorn box?"

"Oh, so you're complaining about the size of my diamond already? I can see you're going to be a hard wife to keep. I'll have you know I saved all my newspaper delivery money for two years to buy that ring for my sister when she turned sixteen."

"You have a sister?"

"Mikayla....She disappeared several years ago. Broke our

family's heart." Adam's eyes squinted in pain at the memory. "No reason that we know of...just didn't return home one night."

"Oh, that's so frightening," Cassidy exclaimed with deepest concern. "I can't imagine your pain."

"Yeah, it's been rough. My parents have been through hell. Not knowing what happened to her rips your guts out. Police...family...friends...we've all searched every way we know how, but never found her, or any reason for her disappearance."

Cassidy didn't say anything for a little while. She turned the ring round and round on her finger. "It's a pretty little ring," she said quietly. "I'll make sure I don't lose it."

Cassidy sucked in a surprised breath when Adam turned into the Lucino acreage and approached his parent's house. She did not expect to behold such immaculate, landscaped grounds where fountains spurt spray high above groomed flower beds and emerald lawns. Oak trees shaded a long, low house with a wide, stone chimney that separated two large windows overlooking the gardens. It was evident that a skilled landscaper and caretaker took excellent care of the property.

Waldo fairly leapt over Cassidy in excitement to get free of the back seat. He ran wild about the yard, much to the dismay of a gray and white cat who was well acquainted with Waldo, and quickly escaped under the doorstep. "Leave Merlin alone," Adam scolded with a shout to Waldo, but the game was on between dog and cat; a game which usually wound up with the pair curled up, sleeping together in their favorite sunny spot on the south side of the house.

Adam's parents hurried down the front steps, which were lined with terra cotta pots bearing brilliant red geraniums. Cassidy felt herself swept into the welcoming arms of his mother before she had barely chance to exit the jeep. "Congratulations! Congratulations!" Adam's mother bubbled in excitement at their engagement, and then hugged her son until Cassidy thought his face would turn blue. Adam glanced back at Cassidy and winked.

Adam's father shook her hand with an extra tender squeeze. "Welcome to our family, Miss Leslie. Adam told us all about you last night, and how you met. I'm so pleased that you are planning to revitalize the Salter River Mansion. It has great possibilities. Our daughter, Mikayla used to love that place. She was always drawing sketches of it."

Cassidy began to panic for a reply, so Adam quickly came to her rescue. His strong arms pulled her against his chest and he kissed her tenderly, as a loving fiancé would. Cassidy had no choice but to allow his caress, and then cast him a scolding glance once his parents weren't looking.

"Cassidy hired me as grounds keeper for her estate," Adam explained in haste. "That's how we met, didn't we, honey." Then he took her hand and headed for the exit. "Sorry! We can't stay long as the plane leaves for Sweden in a few hours and we still have to get though security check."

"Your father knows all the short cuts to the airport," his mother firmly informed her son, finding excuses to hold onto his newfound fiancé a little longer. "Adam says you are interested in history and ancient artifacts, and that you're going to Sweden on an exploration trip. How exciting! Just don't bring home a ghost, dear," she joked.

"She already has one of those," Adam quipped in humor, and Cassidy threw him a giant scowl. Adam simply grinned his crooked smile and gave his mother a loving kiss on the cheek. "We've got to go, Mama. Spoil Waldo for me."

"I always do," she assured him.

Cassidy climbed into the back seat of Adam's father's car, trying to appear cheerful and excited about their trip to Sweden. Just before Adam slid into the front seat beside his father, he hesitated and ran back up the steps to where his mother was waving goodbye. He threw his arms about her and gave her a voluminous hug. A tear clouded Cassidy's eyes for she assumed Adam was thinking if things didn't go well, this may be his last farewell to his mother.

She wished she had also seen her mother before leaving, but there was no time. Five days was quickly turning into four for them to deliver the Harja file. She dug into her purse and withdrew her cell phone. She had to be careful speaking to her mother with Adam's father seated so closely in front of her.

"Hi Mom. No, I'm not at Uncle Raglan's. I'm on my way to the airport. I have an appointment in Sweden...for business...no, not dental...over some of Uncle Raglan's antiques. Yes, it's sudden, but...yes, someone is coming with me...Adam Lucino...Well he knows some contacts over there for me. I'll phone from Sweden when I can, Mom. The plane will be leaving soon...We're going to see Mikkel in Visby...Mikkel in Visby....Yes, write it down. M- I- K- K- E- L. Good! No, I don't have his number. I'll give it to you later. I love you. Goodbye Mom."

She bit back tears, knowing there was a chance she might never return if they met up with the assassins. She realized Adam and herself were not experienced in the criminal world and would be easy prey. If they disappeared, perhaps the name of Mikkel in Visby might give police some clue as to what happened to them. She was comforted to leave the name with her mother. It wasn't much, but it was all she could reveal for the present.

Adam's father turned in the car seat and looked back at her with suspicious eyes. "Would you like to give me your mother's phone number...just in case we need to get in touch with her, or if you'd like us to check up on her while you're gone?"

"Oh, would you please," Cassidy sighed with relief. "I would worry so much less. My father is in the army overseas and hard to contact at times, and Mom is in the Hilltop Senior Complex." She quickly wrote down the particulars for Adam's father and handed him the note. "Make sure Waldo doesn't lose his collar," she added quickly, and Adam's father glanced at her with a puzzled expression. By this time, Adam was jumping into the front car seat beside his father, ready to head for the airport, so nothing more was mentioned about Waldo's collar.

# 7

Adam and Cassidy sat beside each other on the plane, neither conversing for a while. She kept twirling the ring on her finger, wanting to ask more about Mikayla, but not knowing if that would only open up painful wounds for Adam.

Finally, Adam reached over and rested his hand on top of hers to still her fidgeting with the ring. "She would be forty-two years old now."

Cassidy was relieved that he seemed to want to talk about his missing sister. "What was she like?" Cassidy asked with curiosity, wondering if there was any similarity between Mikayla and Adam. She did not have a brother or sister, so the thought of having a sibling intrigued her.

"Well, where should I start? If you think I'm a history buff, you should have known Mikayla," Adam laughed. "She used to drive my mother crazy, dragging rocks and fossils into the house, and hiding them under her bed. She saved her pennies to go into pawn shops and look for mysterious objects...and continued to do so right up to her disappearance."

Adam inhaled a few deep breaths, trying not to appear overly emotional in a plane full of people. "A few years ago, she brought home this unique coin on a string. She was convinced it came from an ancient pirate's treasure. She even wrote to historians to ask about it." He sighed in remembrance. "I thought she was the coolest person."

"I'll bet she thought you were the coolest person when you gave her this ring," Cassidy smiled, and he nodded back in agreement.

"Do you think she might still be alive?" Cassidy quizzed, thinking that Mikayla sounded close-knit with her family, and would not likely vanish without a word on her own accord.

He shrugged his shoulders. "After five years, hope fades a little." He took Cassidy's hand and ran his thumb over the ring on her finger. "The only clue I have that she might still be alive is this ring. It was left in her jewel case when she disappeared. Mikayla never took it off. Never, since the day I gave it to her on her sixteenth birthday. Sometimes I feel her leaving it behind was some kind of message to me, like she was telling me she was still out there."

Cassidy looked at his hand holding hers. She curled her fingers around his palm and gave it a tender squeeze of sympathy. "Well, I think her spirit will always be in this ring, and if she's alive, this ring will bring her back to you."

He turned his face towards her, warmed by her compassion for his loss. He leaned in and touched his lips to her cheek. His kiss was light, like when you touch a warm mitten to your face on a snowy day.

Suddenly, a cane from an elderly woman across the aisle rapped Adam several times on his injured knee. He winced and put his hand over the cane to halt its punishment.

52

"None of that stuff here," the elderly lady scolded.

Adam slowly brushed her cane off his tender knee, inhaled a patient breath, and politely leaned across the aisle to apologize to the woman. "Sorry! We just got engaged and I'm a bit..."

"Twitter-patted! Yes, I know," the lady finished his sentence. "Been there a time or two myself. Keep a lid on it."

With that, Adam leaned back on his seat and glanced over at Cassidy who was trying to hide her embarrassed face against the window. They both burst into spontaneous laughter.

It was not until later in the evening, when lights were dimmed and silence fell within the plane, that Cassidy began to dwell on the strange entrance of Adam into her life. She glanced over at him, asleep with his head turned slightly towards her on the back of the seat. She had seen him almost every day for several years as the ordinary grounds keeper and caretaker of their apartment, but now she contemplated that there was nothing ordinary about Adam Lucino. He had no need to be involved in her life-threatening situation, and yet, here he was, spontaneous to help without any thought of benefit to himself; the kind of stuff that heroes are made of.

Cassidy reached out and attempted to flatten a fly-away whiff of his unruly hair, but it popped back up as if on a spring. She smiled slightly to herself, and decided to accept Adam Lucino as is...which really wasn't too bad of a thing.

The plane landed in Arlanda, Sweden, and Adam hurried off to pick up information and travel maps. They had brought only carry-on backpacks in order to travel light, so she removed her backpack and waited for Adam in an airport restaurant. As Cassidy waited alone at a table, nibbling on a muffin, she could not help but notice a stranger seated across the lounge. He kept turning his head to stare at her. At first, she thought it was not unusual, as people are often drawn to strangers out of curiosity, but after a while, his constant inspection irritated her, and she decided to move away from his prying eyes. Caution made her think to hide her cell phone. She removed her phone out of her purse and turned it off, so it would not ring. Then she slipped the cell beneath the wide headband holding back her hair.

Cassidy seated herself farther down the airport, keeping her eye out for Adam's return. He would not expect her to move from where they first arranged to meet. She anxiously scanned the passing crowd until a man's voice spoke close behind her ear, "Did you lose something, Miss Leslie?" She jerked to attention and felt something dig into her back just below her shoulder blade. Cassidy froze, her imagination automatically suspecting the object to be a gun. She had not expected trouble so soon off the plane.

"Come quietly and you live," the voice whispered low. She glanced back and recognized the man as the one who had been watching her in the previous location. His hat was pulled low, so she could not make out any distinguishing features other than a reddish beard.

She stuttered frantically, "If you want money, I..."

"You have twenty million, I presume!"

When Cassidy shook her head, he gave a devilish grin that chilled her to the bone. "I didn't think so. See that elevator over there. When it's empty, you step into it ahead of me, and if you so much as blink, this knife will find its mark."

Cassidy knew Adam would be looking frantically for her when she was not where they arranged to meet. She wished she had called him on her cell and told him she had moved further down the corridor. One part of her wanted to see him running up to rescue her, but the other part was thankful that he was not present to be captured as well. She slowly pushed her purse and backpack farther under the table with the toe of her shoe, hoping the abductor would not notice. If her belongings were left behind, Adam would realize she was abducted. She rose slowly from her seat and headed for the elevator as instructed, leaving her purse and backpack tucked secretly under the table.

Once the elevator door closed, Cassidy pressed her back against the opposite wall from the stranger. She expected he would not kill her immediately, due to him first needing to torture information out of her. After dwelling on the horrid thought of torture for a few moments, she decided to focus solely on ideas of escape.

She froze against the elevator wall as her abductor patted down her body, carefully checking for any phone or weapon. Having the cell phone undiscovered beneath her headband gave Cassidy a glimmer of hope. If she was given chance alone to call Adam, they could try to figure out a rescue plan.

After leaving the elevator, corridors opened into more corridors until her mind was completely spinning. No opportunities opened for her to escape or call for help without getting stabbed, so she followed his instructions out into the parking lot where a small white car waited. Cassidy was hustled into the back seat beside a handsome young man who looked fresh out of a tennis match with white shirt and shorts, and a tennis racket in a bag by his feet. Blond hair and blue eyes gave her a clue that he was likely of Swedish descent.

"Sorry if Henrik frightened you, but I doubt if you would have accompanied him without fearing for your life. I'm afraid Henrik likes to dramatize the part of a villain. He belongs to a drama club and acting has gone completely to his head." The blond, young man smiled at her, but she did not return his friendliness. After all, they had abducted her at knife-point, and she didn't know what they might have done with Adam. She stared straight ahead without speaking as the three of them drove out of the airport.

.

She could see the back of Henrik's head, as he swung the car into traffic. It had not occurred to her that villains lead perfectly normal lives outside their corrupt dealings. Visioning Henrik acting in drama productions and Lars playing tennis seemed activities that only respectable people would do.

The blond man introduced himself as Lars. "I'm quite aware who you are, Miss Leslie," he informed her with polite mannerism. "It grieves me to have to intercept your plans, but we do have a meeting that was not kept by your uncle." When Cassidy did not reply, he added, "You realize that bills must be paid...one way or another. We all have our jobs to do...We all must earn our pay cheques. Right?"

Cassidy did not open her mouth and focused her eyes out the window, trying to memorize her location should she ever be able to contact Adam on her hidden phone before they discovered it beneath her hair band. Fortunately, a couple imitation flowers concealed the bump of the phone under the band.

"You will find Sweden quite beautiful," Lars continued like an enthusiastic tourist guide, noticing her eyes studying the locations of their travels as their car sped down the highway. "Did you know about sixty percent of Sweden is forest? Very easy to disappear in a forest full of bear and wolves. Notice the Kolen Mountains to the northwest, which divides us from Norway. Very difficult to climb over mountains. To the east of the mountains, you will find coastal plain bordering the Gulf of Bothnia, and south central Sweden is lowland with many lakes. You can swim. Right?" His description of Sweden's topography was laced with death threats, and Cassidy knew he was insinuating any escape would be futile.

When she did not answer, he sighed, "Of course, you are only interested in the Island of Gotland. Right?"

Cassidy was instantly disappointed to find out they knew the Harja file had something to do with Gotland Island. She wondered if they also knew her and Adam were seeking someone called Mikkel on the island. It was difficult to discuss something you knew nothing about with people who thought you were well informed.

Cassidy finally turned to him and asked, "Where are you taking me?" She hoped to extract a fraction of information to tell

Adam. "And I would kindly like to go to a washroom." She hoped if left alone for a few minutes, she could try to contact Adam.

"Aaaah, Henrik. She does have a tongue," Lars laughed joyously. "I was beginning to worry because Ulf might have her tongue removed if it was not of any use."

Cassidy swallowed, but she kept her shoulders squared and her chin up, trying her best not to look intimidated. She turned her face to the window, careful not to miss any hint of location as to where she was.

"I am sure you remember you have a date in Stockholm," Lars smiled, reaching over and boldly resting his hand upon her thigh. "We will be there soon."

Cassidy brushed his hand off her leg with distaste, her eyes sparking with fire. "Not for another two days."

Lars laughed aloud, amused at her spirit. "Stop at *Margaretha's Inn*, Henrik. There are no washroom windows in her establishment, so the door is the only way in or out. Don't try anything foolish, Miss Leslie. I do hate when we have to...dispose of problems. It upsets my tennis swing for a week."

Cassidy closed the washroom door behind her and quickly slipped into a private stall. She pulled the phone out of her head band and dialed Adam's cell in haste. It rang several times, and she heaved an enormous sigh when he answered.

"I only have a moment, Adam," Cassidy talked with rapid information spilling from her lips. "They've abducted me. I'm in a bathroom at Margaretha's Inn, but not for long. They don't know

I have a hidden phone. I think we're heading for Stockholm to a person called Ulf. They mentioned me having to deliver the file there. We're in a white car. I was too nervous to notice the make and license plate. I'm sorry! The drivers are called Lars and Henrik. They seem to know we are interested in Gotland Island. That's all I can tell you for now."

Adam cut in, "The authorities found your purse and backpack, and are holding them and your passport at the airport until you can be located. Look, I'll find the location where we are supposed to make the drop-off in Stockholm. Stall them for a couple days, so I can get my bearings around here. They told us we had five days, so try to make them honor that. Sometimes villains keep a strange sort of honor system."

A pounding knock on the door signaled Cassidy that she had to leave. "I have to go. They're banging on the washroom door. Don't call me. I've turned the ringer off. Stay safe, Adam," she whispered.

"You too," he replied back, and she turned the phone off and slipped it back under her hair band.

# 8

Lars and his driver, Henrik, delivered Cassidy to a large penthouse at the top of a modern, high-rise building. Although she had tried to memorize locations and street signs along the way, the strange Swedish names blurred in Cassidy's memory and she could not remember their spelling or pronunciation.

Cassidy was shown to a long sofa and sat down gingerly, waiting for Ulf to appear. She understood that he was the head of whatever sinister operation they belonged to. When Ulf entered the room, he approached her and held out a hand in friendly greeting. She did not accept his hand for she knew his gesture not to be genuine. They had already warned that they would dispose of her if the file or twenty million was not delivered.

The man they called Ulf was tall and heavily muscled in torso and neck like a football player. He appeared to be about fifty years of age with graying, sandy hair and light blue eyes. When she refused his handshake, his manner immediately turned cold. "Lars has informed me that you feel you have two days left to deliver the map. Save yourself time and energy, Miss Leslie, and then you can return to Canada, safe and sound, and have no more concern for this business. It did not start with you and so you should have no interest in its outcome."

A woman entered the room and appeared surprised to see Cassidy sitting in her living room. Ulf spoke sharply to the woman in Swedish, and she nodded, and turned to leave. Then she turned about as if something had caught her eye. She spoke directly to Cassidy in perfect English, as she walked closer to where Cassidy was seated. "I hope you enjoy your stay in Sweden. It is a beautiful country."

Ulf once again spoke sharply in Swedish to the woman. Cassidy felt the woman was deliberately taunting him by staying longer than he wished. She was dressed in a black, sleeveless dress with a silver chocker necklace that sparkled with expensive diamonds. Her black hair was pulled up into a fall of raven ringlets that allowed the twinkle of precious, diamond ear rings to peep out against the shadows.

The lady looked down on Cassidy, seated timidly on the sofa. Cassidy's knees were shaking and she put her hands over them to still their trembling. The lady's eyes lingered on the tiny gold ring with a blue sapphire stone on Cassidy's finger. "I like your jewelry," the lady said sweetly, leaning over to tap the tiny ring with her index finger. "Your birthstone, I presume?"

"No!" Cassidy replied somewhat shyly. "My...engagement ring." She expected Ulf to explode at their casual chatter, as he had made it quite obvious that he wished the woman to leave them to their business.

The woman's eyes blinked in surprise. Cassidy figured it was because the ring was not the usual expensive diamond for an engagement ring. "Your diamonds are exquisite," Cassidy politely returned the compliment, her voice almost a whisper with Ulf's stare blazing down on the two ladies.

"Yes, Ulf has good taste in diamonds." The woman turned

to smile at Ulf, who was glaring at her with dark, warning eyes. The woman gave her head a slight toss in defiance. "I, myself, would probably have chosen an old coin on a string."

"Your son awaits you by the pool," Ulf informed her coldly. "Best you tend to your business and leave me to mine."

The lady obeyed, but not before she had the last word. "Don't forget to tour the rauks on Gotland Island. That is spelled R-A-U-K. Some rauks resemble people looking out to sea." Then she left them to their business.

Cassidy bit her lip as she waited for whatever evil Ulf had planned for her. Ulf picked up a phone and spoke shortly in Swedish. Within seconds, Lars and Henrik appeared at the door. "Time for another ride," Ulf said, gesturing to the door for her to follow the drivers.

Cassidy figured they would likely try to extract information out of her as soon as they were in some secluded spot. It was a terrible feeling, wondering how brave you are going to be when the time comes to be tortured. It's not something you can prepare for. A high purpose can make pain more bearable, but Cassidy wasn't sure whether the Harja file was a high purpose or not. The only thing that kept her mouth shut was protecting Adam from being found, because Adam didn't deserve any of this trouble.

Cassidy was taken to a warehouse on the outskirts of

Stockholm. As she entered the cold metal building, she could hear wind rattling a loose sheet of metal somewhere. It disturbed pigeons in the rafters, causing them to take constant, sudden flights around the ceiling of the building, and then rest on the rafters once again. It was a foreboding place, and Cassidy realized they had chosen the dejected building to further intimidate her into confessing where the Harja file was. The fact is Cassidy knew very little about the file, only a confusing map on Gotland Island's shoreline. Beyond that, she didn't even know what they were looking for.

"You say two days until you can deliver," Ulf mused thoughtfully, cracking his knuckles as if holding back a desire to wrap them about her throat. "I'm not one to break a deal. We'll give you two days...in this building with nothing but the rats and pigeons to loosen your tongue. We'll check on you in two days. If you're not willing by then to disclose the information we want, then I'm afraid we will have to deal with the matter in rougher terms...but I do hate to resort to broken arms and legs if a more pleasant agreement can be made. Think about it for two days. Henrik...Lars, chain her up."

Henrik grabbed her wrist and she yanked back in resistance, only to have her other wrist snatched by Lars. She was dragged roughly to the east wall where a long, heavy chain hung from a large ring attached to the wall. At the end of the chain was an iron anklet, which Cassidy figured they must have acquired from some medieval dungeon. No doubt, Ulf and his men had used the anklet when chaining up other reluctant victims in the warehouse.

They locked the anklet about her ankle and pocketed the key. Cassidy stood in silence, chained by one foot, which allowed her but a small space to move around in. The only thing that kept her from panicking was knowing that her phone was hidden in her hair band, and there was still the possibility of contacting Adam.

Cassidy knew that Henrik was aware of her arriving in Sweden with Adam, and yet none of the men had mentioned Adam at all. She found this very strange and terrifying. Had they captured and disposed of Adam? She didn't want to even imagine such a thing.

She waited for hours alone in the metal building, too afraid to try the phone in daylight in case they were watching her from a hidden camera somewhere. She had to be sure they could not see her withdraw the phone, and so she waited for nightfall.

Other than the clanging of the loose tin roof, and the cooing of pigeons, all was silent in the large building, which she carefully studied before darkness set in. It appeared to be an old, vacant warehouse or airplane hangar with a row of windows along the top of the walls. She listened carefully but could hear no close traffic, just the sound of distant seagulls. She imagined herself close to a body of water, but then Sweden was a country laden with water sources, so hearing seagulls was probably of little help in giving out her location.

She walked as far as her chain would allow in her small space, fearful to sit down in case rats might creep up and bite her. She could see the rodents scampering by the far wall and knew they were present. "I'll need a dozen rabies and tetanus shots by the time I get out of here," she chattered to herself. After an hour of standing, her legs became weary, and she resorted to sitting down against the wall. She wrapped her skirt tightly about her knees, praying some furry creature would not touch her feet or drop into her hair. For certain, she would freak out if they did.

She withdrew her phone in the darkness, and for a moment held it tenderly to her chest. "Please don't be dead, Adam." She rang his number and he answered instantly on the first ring.

"Oh man, it's good to hear your voice," he expressed with a sigh of relief. "I feared all sorts of things."

"I can't talk long, Adam. I'm afraid the phone battery might go dead. We left Canada in such a hurry that I never charged my phone. I'm chained alone in an old abandoned metal building near water. I could hear seagulls but no traffic. They say they will return in two days to get the file's whereabouts out of me. Until, then, I am chained to the wall."

"Did you notice any landmarks on your way there?"

Cassidy thought for a moment. "So many signs and buildings and roads, all in Swedish. It was all a blur. I was so scared."

"Take some deep breaths. Close your eyes and picture yourself looking out the car window. What do you see?"

"Just people and buildings and buildings...Oh, and a little church. There were gardens of crocuses out front, all different colors like a rainbow. I remember thinking I had never seem such an array of crocus colors where we live. Anyhow, we turned at the church corner and went north into the countryside. I think it was north. I'm not sure. There were cows, and a country road running beside a row of tall trees, and after a while, this big metal building."

"That's excellent. I'll...," Adam's voice cut out.

Cassidy shook the phone frantically. "No! No! Adam, can you hear me?" Her chin dropped on her chest in despair. The phone was dead. It had been her only link to Adam and her only hope for escaping before Ulf returned to torture or murder her. Cassidy tucked the phone back under her hair band, and leaned her head against the wall. Did Adam learn enough information to rescue her before the phone died? She wrapped her arms about herself, shivering in the night's coolness. She knew one thing for sure. If some crawly thing touched her, she was going to scream her head off.

# 9

Adam nearly went frantic when he discovered Cassidy missing at the airport. He rushed to customer service, only to discover that her purse and backpack had been handed in, but no other sign of her. He did not want to alert the police in case going public may force Cassidy's abductors into disposing of her. It was with great relief that he received her phone call from the washroom at *Margaretha's Inn.*

While waiting for a second call, he boarded a bus to Stockholm, where the map was to be delivered. Fortunately, there was a car rental near the bus depot, which not only rented Adam a car, but supplied him with maps of Sweden and Gotland Island. He hoped these road maps would be valuable to him in finding Cassidy, and escaping to Gotland Island to find a contact named Mikkel.

As the day progressed, he set about memorizing the main streets of the city, locating where the drop-off was supposed to be, and learning transportation available to Gotland Island. He thought to try and locate Mikkel, but he did not know who the man was. Perhaps Mikkel was only interested in the value of the Harja file, and would sacrifice Cassidy to get it.

Adam could do nothing but work on an escape route for Cassidy and himself, should he be able to get her away from Ulf's clutches. He knew it would be a slim possibility, as he had no weapon, no understanding of the Swedish language, and not a clue as to where she was presently located. All he could do was hope for a miracle.

As he waited anxiously for her second call, he had time to think about Cassidy Leslie. He never anticipated that they would be drawn together in such a terrifying twist of events. They barely knew each other a couple days ago, and yet now, here they were in Sweden with Cassidy kidnapped, and him searching desperately to find her before Ulf took her life. His mother used to tell him that life was like driftwood. You just never know how far it will take you or what shore you're going to wash up on.

An overwhelming sigh of relief escaped from Adam's chest when his cell phone rang, and he heard Cassidy's voice. Fresh hope arose as he listened to her describe her whereabouts to the metal warehouse. It was nightfall, but he was sure if he found a pub open, there would be English speaking tourists who would recognize the location of the little church with the crocus gardens.

As luck would have it, one English speaking tourist in the pub had seen the little church, and even showed Adam photographs of it on her camera. She circled the church's location on Adam's map, and he hurried off in search of the landmark. Adam soon discovered the small stone church, snuggled behind colorful beds of anemones like a pot of gold at the end of the rainbow.

He traveled in the direction that Cassidy thought they had driven, trying with difficulty to distinguish landmarks in the dark. He eventually arrived at a location where a small dirt road branched off the highway. The trail wound beside a pasture, as Cassidy had described. Cattle were lying down and barely visible in the dark, but he could distinguish a tall row of trees protruding into the skyline. Adam's excitement grew as he hurried down the country road, hopeful that this was the correct path leading to the warehouse. He turned the lights off on the car and let only the glow from the moon guide his path.

Moonlight reflected off the huge metal shed, making the building luminous in the dark. Adam parked the rental car off the trail, concealing it behind bushes in case Ulf and his men might return. He walked slowly and cautiously towards the metal building, keeping to the shadows of trees as much as possible. His head constantly turned backward to check that he was alone. There were no windows in the long metal building low enough for him to peer into, so he had to chance opening the door, and hope no one stood on the opposite side with a gun aimed at his head. As Adam gingerly opened the door, the moon slithered a long silver ribbon across to Cassidy, who jumped to her feet in fright.

"It's me," Adam spoke quickly to calm her. "Let's get you out of here."

He hurried across the shed and Cassidy held her hands over her mouth to smother a flood of relieved tears. He held her close for a moment, as she sobbed on his chest, relieved at being found and seeing him unharmed. Finally, she stopped sobbing, embarrassed that she had completely unraveled in his arms. She tried to wipe the tears from her cheeks with dirty hands, and wound up looking even more pitiful.

Adam's voice made the victory short lived. "I...I think we

better not celebrate yet...I forgot about the anklet. No key!"

Cassidy was shocked back into reality and fresh panic set into her. "I tried to get my foot out, but I can't..." She held her foot out, and a ring of red, skinned flesh showed evidence of long hours of trying to squeeze her foot out of the anklet without success. "How did you get here?" she asked shakily.

"By rental car...Say, maybe there's a tire rod in the trunk." He ran out of the building and returned quickly with every tool he could find in the car. None could break the strong, iron anklet's lock or chain links. He sadly viewed the ring of chaffed skin and blood around her ankle. "I can see there's no use trying anymore to slip your foot out," he said, taking note of her fruitless efforts. "Maybe I'll try to trip the lock."

He withdrew a small jackknife and inserted it into the lock, but no amount of twisting and turning could open the lock. He sat back in despair and sighed, "It works in the movies all the time." He pondered for a few moments. "I passed a farm nearby. Most farmers keep saws that can cut through metal. I'll see if they have one that will saw through this chain."

Cassidy looked at him with enormous frightened eyes. She did not think she could bare to be left alone in the warehouse for one more second. Her heart raced once again with the fear of not being able to escape before Ulf returned.

"They might keep guard dogs," Cassidy warned, trying once more to squeeze her foot out of the anklet. "Nobody is going to trust a stranger banging on their door in the middle of the night. Even if they understood English, they would think you were nuts, needing a saw to cut the chain off a girl imprisoned in a warehouse...Maybe they know Ulf and keep this warehouse for him on their land. We can't trust anyone. They'll set their dogs on you for sure."

Adam Lucino sighed. "Then I guess I have no choice but to steal...borrow...a saw...and don't worry. If I can handle Waldo, I can handle any dog smaller than a horse."

Adam disappeared out the door and back into the darkness. She heard his car drive away and spoke with a discouraged voice that only the pigeons heard. "Yes, but Waldo doesn't know he's a dog."

~⌇~

Adam parked the rental vehicle a distance away from the nearby farmyard and gingerly approached on foot. He surveyed the buildings, partly visible in the dark by a pole-light in the center of the yard. He figured a small shed to the outskirts might be a tool shed, but when he opened the door, only a pair of friendly goats greeted him with a few gentle bleats. Adam shut the door quickly and approached another shed. This time, he successfully found a few tools he hoped would cut the chain free.

So far, no dog had signaled his intrusion, and his confidence mounted until he crossed the path of a pair of sleeping geese. With flapping wings and an array of hissing and loud honking, the largest gander turned into a formidable road block. Adam saw lights flick on in the house and took a running leap at the goose, flying over it and into the shadows of the bush before the farmer exited the house. As he escaped to the car, the disturbed barnyard came to life with an array of livestock sounds, accompanied by a dog who finally wakened to bark, and a farmer yelling warnings into the night in a language it was best Adam couldn't understand.

Adam returned to Cassidy with a saw and an acetylene torch. "We'll try the blow torch first," he told her. Adam laid his jacket over her foot, and held the nozzle of the torch about an arm's length away from her ankle, so that the heat would not burn her leg. The hot torch soon heated the chain to glowing red. Adam sat the acetylene torch down and grabbed a tire iron and pried the hot chain-link apart.

Cassidy felt a volume of relief at being freed from the wall, but she was not free of the anklet and a length of dangling chain. "How am I going to hide this from people?" she half cried. "Someone will report me to the police for sure if they see me dragging a chain like an escaped convict."

"No time to worry about that now. I'll bring the saw with us and cut the chain off later," Adam quickly assured her, not wanting to waste any time in escaping from the warehouse. "Best we get out of here before they come back to check on you."

Cassidy stood in her dirt-stained, pastel pink skirt, holding up the chain connected to the anklet like someone holding a snake with distaste.

Adam saddened to see her looking so desolate. "Don't touch the end where it's hot," he warned quickly. "I have my backpack in the car. You can slip into one of my sweats later, and pull the chain up your pant leg. Then no one will notice the chain...but first, we've got to get out of here."

The couple drove down the first dirt road that branched away from the warehouse. Adam grabbed a map from the back seat. "The car rental gave me maps. We'll hit for Nynashamn, where we'll try to catch a ferry to Visby. Nynashamn is south of Stockholm. The rental told me a ferry sails to Gotland at midnight, but we've missed that, so we'll have to wait there until a ferry departs. Let's hope Ulf doesn't arrive while we're waiting."

"I could try to disguise myself a bit," Cassidy suggested. "I'll tie my hair back and pull the hood of your sweater over my head. With men's sweat pants, and your sweater, maybe I can appear as a boy if I keep my head down. We better not take the car on the ferry. Too noticeable. Likely, we can rent bicycles on the island." Cassidy removed her cell phone from beneath her hair band, as the battery was dead, and slipped it into his backpack while searching for suitable clothes to wear for a disguise.

"Good idea," Adam agreed, "And if Ulf asks the ferry who crossed, they'll only remember us as two men folk. I rented the car for a week, so it can stay here at the ferry docks as a getaway car in case we need it later."

# 10

The old city of Visby was known for being a major trade center since medieval times, and was surrounded by an ancient fortress wall, which awed the young couple. Forty-four towers and numerous gateways strung along the 3.4 km long wall, once built by German tradesmen to save the prosperous trading center from plundering during the 1288 Civil War. Cobblestone streets and alleys wound amongst many medieval churches, some restored and still in use. History-keen Adam and Cassidy were fascinated by the ancient stone, wooden and limestone houses with attractive reed rooftops. For a while, their quest to find the Harja file seemed lost in their distraction of historic Gotland Island.

During their wait for the ferry, Adam had successfully sawed off the chain link closest to the iron anklet on Cassidy's foot, but there was no removing the anklet without the key. Cassidy was still in need of concealing the anklet with long pants, so they stopped at a store in Visby where Cassidy quickly purchased lady's slacks and a clean blouse. She also bought a scarf and looped it over and under all around the anklet to make a soft barrier between the iron and her sore ankle. "Perhaps I'll start a new fashion statement," she kidded.

After biking around Visby for half the morning, looking for a sign with Mikkel on it, Cassidy dismounted her rental bike and sat beside the road with dejected shoulders. She rubbed her sore ankle and complained, "It's useless. We'll never find Mikkel this way." She tossed a pebble aimlessly at a larger stone and watched it bounce off and rebound back to her feet for a second disheartened throw.

"The phone directory shows hundreds of people with Mikkel as a first and a last name, so I don't know how your uncle thought we could ever locate the fellow," Adam grumbled in frustration. "Your Uncle Raglan sure had a knack for riddles."

"Well, I think there's simply a clue that we are missing."

"Guess we'll just have to put our heads together and follow the map that we memorized," Adam decided. "It's the only thing we have to lead us to whatever these thieves are looking for."

Cassidy glanced over at him. "I'm not sure I want to find what they're looking for, if it's worth killing people over. And I'm afraid I am slowly forgetting what was on the map. I know it showed a road north of Visby towards the coast line. Perhaps we can bike there for a starter and things might refresh my memory."

Adam looked out across the countryside, dotted with country churches and rural limestone farmhouses. Grey, curly-haired sheep grazed on poor vegetation nearby, and in the distance, the cry of ocean birds echoed across the island. It was a peaceful place, the old still evident amongst the new. "I agree." he said with fresh enthusiasm. "Let's hit for the sea...and a place to eat. I'm starved."

Ulf ate his breakfast in a frustrated manner, stabbing his fork into his food as if spearing fish in a stream. His wife sat abreast of him on the other side of the table, pretending not to notice his perplexed temperament. She buttered a piece of tangy, rye sourdough bread, and commented, "The lady in the living room yesterday seemed very nice."

"And very stupid," Ulf snarled. Then he wiped his mouth on a napkin and rose from the table, kicking his chair out of the way as he strode off in long, stiff strides. He put a phone to his ear. "Check on her this morning, Lars. One night with the rats should be enough to make her talk."

His wife overheard and winced sadly, but said nothing, for she was not blind to the ill dealings of her husband. "I promised to take your son to the beach today," she informed him casually. "He wants to search for pieces of coral."

Ulf impatiently waved permission for her to go to the beach, as he dialed another number on his phone. "Go...Go! Take Erica with you."

She quickly took her son's hand and left the room. Once alone, she pressed a buzzer to contact Erica. The woman entered in a navy uniform, starched stiff as cardboard. Ulf's wife handed her bodyguard a sum of money and requested, "Could you go shopping and find me a pair of shoes to match my blue gown for tonight? Ulf is having a few friends over and wants me to look my best. I think I will just spend the day on the beach with my son...Oh, and buy yourself...a brooch or something." She was thinking that any bling on Erica's frigid uniform would be an improvement.

"You know I cannot accept gifts." Erica snapped sharply, her square chin slightly uplifted at the offer. "But I will take my time shopping, madam. We both should return at the same hour, I should think...six o'clock sharp." Erica whirled about and clumped out of the room in heavy, black oxford shoes. Ulf's wife didn't say a word. She was in complete shock that Erica had agreed to leave her and the boy unchaperoned for the day. Ulf always ordered Erica to shadow her everywhere.

Ulf's wife and son were long gone to the beach by the time Ulf learned from Lars and Henrik that Cassidy had escaped from the steel shed. Ulf was furious with his men. "Fools!" he screamed at them. "The only way he'd find her is if she had a phone to call him. Some body-search you must have done. I thought you had this partner of hers under surveillance the minute they got off the plane."

"Matts was supposed to, sir," Lars explained with frustration. "Henrik and I were with the lady. Matts lost him in traffic after the guy rented a car, but he did get the license plate number from the car rental boy, after a bit of persuasion. We found the car abandoned at the ferry docks. Looks like they crossed over to Gotland Island early this morning."

"I'll ride with Matts, and we'll check every road out of Visby until we find the fools," Ulf ordered. "Forget the five day time limit...The sea can have them."

Ulf and his three men crossed the ferry with two cars, and learned that two men had rented bicycles immediately upon getting off the ferry earlier that morning. They assumed the two were Cassidy and Adam, so the four men fanned out from Visby, hoping to locate the couple traveling at a slower pace on bicycles.

Cassidy and Adam stopped at a small restaurant on their journey to the northern coast. She noticed Adam rubbing his knee, although he had not uttered a word of complaint. She realized that cycling was probably not the best action for his injured leg. She excused herself from the table and approached one of the servers. Soon the conversation involved two others, and Adam rose to join them, puzzled as to what was going on.

Cassidy assured Adam everything was fine. "I'm just buying you a thank you gift." She turned to a young man in the restaurant. "First I see if it can start. Then the cash." The young man nodded in agreement, and left the building.

The teenager returned shortly with a small motorcycle that showed much former use. Dents and scratches covered much of the bike, but the tires appeared sound and he even indicated to her that it had a full tank of gas. "Bike very good," he assured Cassidy with a Swedish accent. "I do tricks." He gestured with his hands to interpret flying off ramps and flipping in the air. "Strong frame. Good tires...When you are done, I buy back...half price."

"Half price?" Cassidy shrieked.

The young man shrugged his shoulders. "Good deal for a beat up old bike."

Cassidy threw a disgusted look at the smiling and devious

young man, but she thought of Adam's leg and agreed. "Okay! And I trust you will return the rental bikes for us like you promised." The young man nodded in agreement and she turned to Adam. "My purse is at the airport. I need to borrow money from you to buy the motorbike."

"So I have to pay for my own gift?" Adam said sarcastically, and handed the young man payment for the motorcycle. "I feel married already."

Adam was like a child receiving a gift on Christmas morning. "My Uncle Romano in Winnipeg sells bikes," he told Cassidy with a triumphant smile. "I was practically born on one of these things." He hopped on the bike and beckoned Cassidy to climb on behind him. Adam revved the engine, enjoying the sound of its deep throaty roar. Cassidy assumed there was something about the deafening thunder of a motor that stirs the lion-heart in every male.

Not long after Cassidy and Adam left the restaurant, a shiny black car pulled up. Ulf and his man, Matts, stepped out and approached the staff, walking slow and deliberate with an intimidating air. The workers knew who Ulf Lindberg was. His shady character as an illegal treasure-hunter was well known in Sweden, even though no crime had been pinned on him. Ulf Lindberg dealt in a world where people purchase stolen artifacts for their private collections. Everybody knew it.

The locals on Gotland Island regarded Ulf as a modern-day pirate, and so their mouths were close-lipped about Cassidy and Adam. No one breathed a word about the young couple stopping at the restaurant or buying a motorcycle, but their nervous, diverting eyes did not go unnoticed by Ulf. He quickly surmised the locals hid the truth. He had no time to scare the truth out of them, so returned to the car. The men aimed down the highway with fresh gusto, feeling they would soon catch up to the pair, whom they believed to be traveling more slowly on bicycles.

As Cassidy and Adam raced down the road on the small motorcycle, Cassidy noticed that no billboards littered the sides of the road. Only an occasional, modern wind turbine disturbed the sleepy scenery of numerous medieval churches and historic remnants, draped in grape vines. Cassidy relaxed for the first time in weeks as they passed groves of mulberry, walnut, and peach trees. She rested the side of her face against Adam's back, desiring peace and sleep.

Adam did not give her long for idleness. He stopped the motorcycle for a fraction of a minute, withdrew a map and brochure from his backpack, and handed them to Cassidy. Then he continued at a fast pace down the road again, asking her to direct him to the shoreline, and read any information that might help them in their knowledge of Gotland Island.

Cassidy pressed the brochure against his back to prevent the wind from whipping it from her hands. "It says here that Gotland Island is famous for discoveries of ancient coins of gold, silver and copper, and that more than 700 coin treasures have been found. The largest silver treasure of over 80 kilos, dating back to the Viking Age, was found on northern Gotland in 1999. Wow! Do you think the Harja file might have something to do with a treasure?"

Adam kept his eye on the road and shouted back, "Maybe, but I still think it has something to do with runes. Why else would they call it the Harja File?"

Cassidy continued reading the information on the brochure. "It says Gotland is known as *'The World's Treasury'*, as over 140,000 coins have been found here, due to the place being a major trading center back in medieval times. Many of the treasures are in the National Museum of Stockholm, but they originated on Gotland Island. Arab, Greek, Roman and other coins can be found to this day all over the island."

"What about runes?" Adam asked, still believing strongly that the file would not be named Harja unless involving runes.

"Let's see!" Cassidy mused, as she explored the brochure further. "Runes! Runes! The brochure says most rune stones are found on the mainland of Sweden, but one of the oldest runes was found on a spear edge on Gotland, dating as early as the 3rd century."

Cassidy paused in her reading to turn her head slightly backward to check on upcoming traffic, and saw a fast approaching car with Ulf's face clearly visible in the front window. "Oh no!" she cried. "It's them."

Adam took a hasty peek in his rear-view mirror to confirm her statement, and yelled, "Hang on tight." He aimed the motorcycle off the road and lifted the bike in a flying leap over a ditch. Then, like a deer fleeing a hunter, he headed for the safety of some unknown destination.

Ulf and Matts were not discouraged. They continued at intense speed, and also cleared the ditch, car windows shattering like ice crystals as the vehicle hammered the ground on the other side of the ditch. Adam tried his best to shake the determined criminals, winding in and out of farm yards and over barren hilly moors. He then hit for meadowland, hoping to entice their car into a wetter area where Ulf's car might get stuck. It was difficult to gain speed with two riders on the small motorcycle, so Adam knew one of them had to dismount.

Adam ducked behind a column of trees beside a pond. "We can't escape with both of us on the bike," he panted, breathing hard. "I'll be back. Hide in the culvert that we passed near that ditch a ways back." Then he took off, and Cassidy knelt down in the leafy growth, as the car sped by on Adam's tail. As soon as the car disappeared, she ran across the damp meadow grass and crawled into a culvert beneath the road. She was thankful that the culvert was free of water, and leaned her back against the curved side, curling her body like a crescent moon.

Cassidy waited for hours, fearful of what Ulf and his men would do with Adam if they caught up to him. She prayed the old motorbike would hold up with all the punishment it must be taking. She trembled and tried not to count the spiders and bugs that accompanied her in the tunnel. After a while, her back felt cramped in the crescent moon position, so she stretched out on her side, feeling like a gopher in an underground tunnel.

"Did Gotland Island have skunks?" she suddenly wondered, nervously watching both ends of the culvert for unwelcome intruders. Someone once told her that there were no skunks in Great Britain, so she hoped there were none on Gotland Island, as well. Such insignificant information can be important when you are lying in the middle of a corridor for wild animals. Rats, well, she figured every country had rats, and they had better not be taking a shortcut through this culvert.

The danger of being hunted by Ulf had allowed little time for thoughts of anything but trying to stay alive. Her and Adam had been too busy checking out shadows to think about feelings, but now in the quietness of the culvert, Cassidy clung to whatever good qualities she could think of about Adam. He was someone who wouldn't let her down. She was sure of it. He would come back for her.

She recalled her first opinion of Adam, and smiled to herself. Even his unruly hair set him apart from the ideal. Her first perception of him had not drummed up desire or passion, but now...she would give anything to see his crooked smile at the end of that culvert, and feel his secure arms around her.

Cassidy remembered someone saying, *"Perception is a powerful thing. It doesn't change unless a person is knocked off their feet by a significant event. Only then does it reset their judgment."* Cassidy decided it was certainly true in the case of her perception of Adam.

She returned to her crescent moon position and rested her head on folded arms upon her knees. Cassidy closed her eyes, and drifted off to sleep, as she had not slept since being on the plane to Sweden.

Hours later, Adam's welcome voice echoed through the culvert shaft. "Anybody home?" Cassidy couldn't scramble out of the culvert fast enough. She collapsed into his welcome arms as he pulled her from the culvert.

Adam brushed a cob web from her hair while they sat in the grass to rest for a few minutes. Cassidy looked around and beheld colorful wild orchids waving in the sweet smelling meadow grass about them. She longed to fling herself down amongst the blooms, stretch out her arms and lie beside Adam like a sun-warmed pebble on the beach, but there was no time for such tranquility.

"Time to go", he said quietly with a tired sigh, for he was exhausted from the strenuous bike ride in escaping Ulf. "They saw me on the bike alone, and know I will backtrack to pick you up." Without further hesitation, they mounted the motorcycle and aimed for the northern coast line.

# 11

"I lost them in an old farm yard," Adam explained with amusement over his shoulder, as they traveled down a winding country road. "Their car ran into a piece of machinery hidden in some tall weeds. I looked back and all I saw was steam coming from their radiator, and two men wildly waving their arms like teenagers at a rock concert."

Cassidy and Adam stopped their motorcycle after a time and spread the car rental maps upon the ground. They tried to recall from memory what had been on the treasure map.

"We need to find something to do with three daggers, which were shown at the starting point on the map," Adam informed her, "and some strange figurine looking out to sea."

"The rauks," Cassidy burst out. "The rauks. She said don't forget to see the rauks. They look like people looking out to sea."

"Who and what are you talking about?" Adam quizzed, his face full of puzzlement.

"The lady at Ulf's residence. I'm sure she was his wife because they spoke of a child. He didn't want her to speak to me, but she did...in perfect English, and I had a feeling she was...defiant somehow, like she was obeying his orders and yet, revolting against him at the same time. Weird! She even spelled

R-A-U-K out for me. What are they?"

"They're limestone rocks along the coast," Adam explained quickly, "weathered into stone column formations. The Swedish call them sea-stacks or *rauks*. Let's hit for them. It can't hurt to check them out."

The couple were not alone on the coastline where many rauks resembled figurines looking out to sea. Tourists dotted the landscape and Cassidy and Adam quickly scanned their faces as they passed by, hoping not to discover Ulf's men amongst them.

Suddenly, Cassidy noticed Ulf's wife sitting quietly on a rocky shelf with her young son. The lady rose, as if she had been waiting for them, and walked slowly towards Adam, making sure he was who she thought he was. The woman nodded hello to Cassidy, whom she recognized as the lady in her living room in Stockholm. Cassidy nodded back, recognizing the woman as Ulf's wife, but Adam recognized the lady as someone else.

"Mikayla!" Adam's voice escaped in a whisper, and then his face teared up in pain and bewilderment at recognizing his sister, whom he had presumed dead for five years. "Why? How?"

She threw her arms about his neck and tucked her head into his shoulder. "Oh, dear Adam! How I have longed to see you all these years...but we must not stay long in the open. Ulf and his men might see us together. We can't stay here."

Cassidy pointed towards her little boy placing small rocks in his pail. "Ulf's son?"

Mikayla nodded in haste, "Yes! He is Ulf and my son. Ulf uses the child as a way to keep me silent. He has threatened the boy's life many times if I try to contact anyone...and he means it."

"How in heavens did you get mixed up with such a man?" Adam asked almost angrily, yet feeling so relieved to find his sister alive. "We would have helped you."

"I could say nothing. At first, he threatened your lives. Then the child's...It started out so innocently," Mikayla tried to explain, her eyes darting about as she spoke, hoping no one recognizable would chance into view. "I simply drew a picture of Raglan Leslie's Victorian mansion. I was always sketching that magnificent old place. I thought he might like a sketch, so I knocked on his door one day and offered it to him. He insisted on paying me for it, and gave me that old coin on a string. Remember?"

"I remember," Adam said. "I thought you found it in a pawn shop."

"No, it was from Raglan Leslie. He said it was from a pirate's treasure, and that his wife found the coin on their honeymoon on the shores of the Baltic Sea. He said he was giving it to me for safe keeping, so the pirates wouldn't get it. I thought he was simply an old man telling pirate tales at the time. I didn't realize he was actually hiding a real artifact with me."

Mikayla knelt beside her son and hurried him into gathering up his shovels to put in his pail. "I started inquiring about the authenticity of the coin online, and suddenly I received an answer from a man who wanted to meet me and see the coin. He asked a hundred questions about Mr. Leslie and exactly where the coin was found, but I knew little to tell the man, so then he wanted to see Raglan Leslie."

She shook her head at her foolishness in trusting the stranger. "I was a gullible fool to believe in the man. Ulf Lindberg told me to keep our meeting secret because of business reasons, and to not even tell my family until he had returned to his country. I agreed, as I didn't see any harm in it at the time. I should have guessed something was wrong, but he was very knowledgeable about ancient treasures, so I found him fascinating to talk to."

Mikayla picked up her son, anxious to find a more protective spot. "The next day, Ulf met me at Raglan Leslie's house, but Mr. Leslie was very defensive about giving any information about the coin. He nearly threw Ulf out the door. I have always regretted not getting back to apologize to Mr. Leslie before he died. He entrusted the coin to me and I let him down. I should have spoken to him before I went looking for answers about the coin."

The foursome hurried their pace towards the rauks farther down the shore. Mikayla pulled her wide brimmed hat lower over her face, so no one would recognize her. She had come to this beach for five years and it was very possible to run into people who would recognize her as Ulf Lindberg's wife. She did not want word to get back to Ulf that she was alone without Erica, and speaking to strangers.

"Ulf's personality switched to evil the moment he didn't get any information," Mikayla explained as they approached the rauks. "He ordered me into a taxi, took me home and warned me to return with the coin or he'd kill my parents. The taxi driver, unfortunately, overheard Ulf's threat to me, so after I brought Ulf the coin from our house, Ulf forced the taxi driver to take us down to the pier. There, he shot poor Simco and kicked his body off the dock. I was truly sick. Simco didn't deserve that. He was just a kindly old taxi driver who would never accept a tip from me.

*"You save my tips for me,"* he'd say, *"cause I'll just spend 'em on cigarettes. When you gets to a thousand, I'm gonna take a trip to Las Vegas, and bring you back a million."*

Mikayla bit her lips to hold back painful tears, as she spoke of the kind taxi driver. "He always wore this old cap with Simco written across the front. I don't know if that was his real name or not. He never had any family that I know of. Likely wasn't even missed."

Adam rested a comforting hand on her shoulder, but there were no words to erase the pain of witnessing Simco's murder. Mikayla looked across at the sea waves, approaching the shore like frothy, storm clouds. For the past five years, her life had been like the tide, hope for escape coming in and then hope receding again. It was hard for her to believe that maybe this time, there was chance of escaping Ulf Lindberg.

Cassidy and Adam followed Mikayla toward the rauks, listening carefully to her tale. "I told Ulf just to take the coin and go, but he felt I knew more about Raglan Leslie's secret than I was telling. That's why he kept me captive all these years, forced a marriage and child to stop me from escaping...until he finds the treasure...then I am not sure what my husband intends to do with us. Likely the same fate as Simco."

Mikayla stopped and bent down to pick up a small rock with a fossil in it. She handed it to her son. "Look, Mikkel. From the sea!" She rubbed her son's hair fondly and looked out onto the white capped waves swallowing the shoreline. She did not notice the sudden shock that rippled across Adam and Cassidy's faces at the mention of her son's name.

"You know," Mikayla laughed, "people are so busy looking for pirate treasure on Gotland Island, that they overlook the wonder of discovering these prehistoric animals. This island is a paradise for fossil-hunters, especially the southern sandy shoreline where lime enriched soil has preserved many marine fossils. Mikkel and I have become quite the treasure hunters."

Cassidy and Adam could not restrain themselves one more second. They both burst out her son's name in unison. "MIKKEL!"

Mikayla looked at them with a huge frown. "Yes, this is Mikkel."

Cassidy was overjoyed at the mention of Mikayla's son's name. "Uncle Raglan left a message, saying, *"Go to Visby. Find Mikkel"*. I guess he knew that if we found Mikkel, we would find you. I didn't realize Uncle Raglan knew about your kidnapping, or the birth of your child. I am surprised he didn't confide in me, or at least in my father."

Mikalya nodded sadly. "I think your uncle feared for my life if he said a word. I'm sure he realized that the moment Ulf knew the whereabouts of the treasure I would be disposed of. So he kept Ulf guessing. Your uncle was quite imaginative in ways to stall Ulf, like saying only his deceased wife knew the treasure's location, and that he had to go through her things to try and find a clue. He used to drive Ulf wild, delaying the search for different reasons. Raglan Leslie prolonged my life to his last dying breath. Bless him!"

Adam reached out and took the four year old from Mikayla's arms. "Hi little fellow," Adam smiled, and the boy smiled shyly back, his wild raven hair closely resembling his uncle's disheveled locks.

"Ulf believes Mr. Leslie's coin came from a pirate treasure buried on Gotland Island about a thousand years ago," Mikayla explained, inhaling a deep breath to begin her tale. "A Viking pirate, nicknamed "Skully" was rumored to possess a medieval dagger from his ancient ancestors. The blade is supposedly inscribed with runic language. Such a runic artifact would be an unimaginable find, and would bring Ulf a fortune on the black market, far more than the treasure itself. Captain Skuli Hanns considered the dagger to have magical powers. It is said he confiscated an enormous booty of gold and silver articles from churches along the shores of France, and decided to leave the rune-engraved dagger with his plunder, believing it would guard the treasure until his safe return. Skully was killed at sea shortly after wards, and people have searched for centuries, hoping to find Skully's last treasure with the runic dagger."

"How does anyone know the coin you have came from Skully's treasure?" Adam asked. "There were many pirates who stopped merchant ships heading to trade in those ancient days."

"Yes, that's true," Mikayla agreed. "Pirates looted across western and eastern Europe as far east as Afghanistan. Captain Skully was known to sail down Russia's long rivers to the Middle East. He had a habit of "pecking" each coin three times with knife marks, once on the upper left hand side on the front of the coin, and twice on the lower right hand side on the back of the coin, to check on whether they were genuine or counterfeits made of lead. The coin given to me had those precise pecking marks."

"So who named the treasure the Harja file?" Cassidy questioned. "Back in Skully's day, the Vimose Comb hadn't been discovered yet."

"I think at first it was a code name that Mr. Leslie and Ulf used when talking about the treasure in case others overheard their conversations," Mikayla answered. "Eventually, the map just became known as the Harja file. The word 'treasure' gets everyone's adrenalin flowing, so they decided to call it a file in case the word, "treasure" slipped out."

Cassidy listened with keen interest to Mikayla's pirate tales. She turned to look out on the Baltic Sea. "I feel like I have gone back in time, looking out on the sea where merchant ships and pirates once sailed. Even I get excited at the mention of treasure."

## "Sails on the Horizon"
## Painting by Verna Elliott Hutlet

*"I feel like I have gone back in time, looking out on the sea where merchant ships and pirates once sailed."*

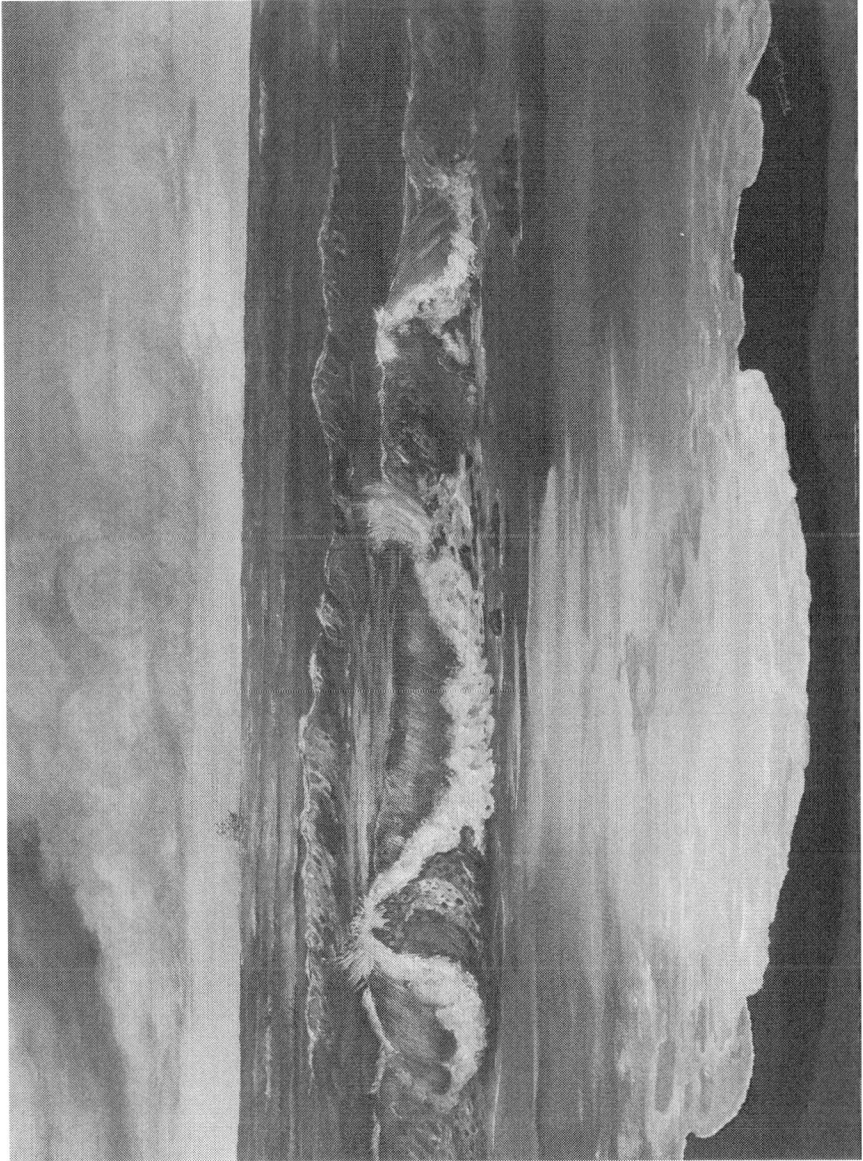

# 12

Mikayla enjoyed talking about the history of Gotland Island. She had grown very fond of the island and its folklore. "It's possible that the runic sword is a true story," Mikayla added, "or part of a true story that became stretched into a legend. There certainly are treasures buried here. In 2007, a thousand year old Viking treasure was dug up in a vegetable garden on Gotland, holding money and foreign currency from present-day England, Ireland, Germany, Iraq and Uzbekistan. So finding treasures is a possibility."

Thrilled with the island's history, Mikayla continued with an excited pitch to her voice. "Pirates also made a fortune with *danegeld;* protection money paid by district rulers to keep Vikings from attacking. Sometimes the pirates had so much coin that they buried it like deposit boxes until needed. Some pirates never lived to return for their treasures. Maybe others forgot where they buried it, or had so much, they never needed it. I am sure Skully's treasure is out there somewhere."

Adam lowered Mikkel to the ground, as the boy insisted on looking for more rocks containing fossils. "Time for you and Mikkel to get out of sight where our modern-day pirate can't find you. Do you have any person you can trust?"

Mikayla shook her head. "No one. Ulf Lindberg made sure of that. Erica, my bodyguard, helped me get away alone today...but I'm not sure of her loyalty. I think she is secretly meeting a man whom Ulf dislikes, and her letting me go without escort today was for her benefit, not mine. In a pinch, I think she would save her skin and favor Ulf."

"Then trust no one. Is there any place for you to hide for the remainder of today?"

"The Lummelunda caves!" Mikayla answered without hesitation. "They have guided tours for those wanting to see the cave rooms. We can spend a lot of time there, blending in as tourists, looking at the fossils and stalactites until you return for us." She turned to hurry away with Mikkel.

"Wait!" Cassidy called. She slid the petite gold ring with the sapphire stone off her finger and held it out to Mikayla in the palm of her hand. "I believe this ring belongs to you."

Mikayla hesitated in accepting the ring. "But you said it was your engagement ring."

Adam's eyebrows arched in surprise at Cassidy's reference to Mikayla's ring as their engagement ring, so she quickly set the record straight. "Only for a short period of time. Sort of like a test drive before you buy a car."

"Then you should keep it, if the trial period went well," Mikayla teased with a mischievous twinkle in her eye.

Cassidy shook her head. "We're not compatible."

Adam's face winced, so she kindly added, "We both want to sit by the window in the plane."

Mikayla laughed out loud, perhaps the first laugh she had expressed freely for years. Mikayla slipped the ring on her own finger and turned to smile at Adam. "I left this ring behind in case I never returned, so you would have a part of me....Well, I'm back, little brother."

Adam smiled and gave her and Mikkel an enormous hug before stepping back and squaring his shoulders. "Go quickly and don't look back, Mickie. You're free."

Mikayla grasped Mikkel's hand and they ran like two liberated seabirds taking flight. She did not look back in case the dream evaporated.

Cassidy and Adam walked amongst the rauks, trying to decide which one was used on Skully's map. Many resembled figurines looking out to sea, so it was difficult to choose. Finally, Cassidy bent over and rubbed her aching ankle. "Man, this iron anklet feels like it weighs a ton, and it's rubbed my ankle raw. I don't know if I can walk another step with it on."

Adam knelt down and examined her sore ankle. He rose to his feet and walked over to a family seated nearby. Cassidy saw a lady rustle in her purse and then hand Adam a little tube of something. He then returned to Cassidy and squeezed a tube of suntan oil into his hand. He oiled her foot until it gleamed like a slippery seal. "Now let's try to squeeze your foot out," Adam requested. "Pretend you are taking off my engagement ring."

Cassidy wriggled and twisted her foot as hard as she could. "Keep going," Adam encouraged. "I think it's coming, bit by bit." Adam kept dropping more oil between the anklet and her foot as she twisted it back and forth. It was a painful procedure, but Cassidy closed her eyes tightly and kept trying until her foot popped out like a cork in a bottle. They cheered in unison, and then she quickly scrambled to her feet, discarding the anklet.

A child passed by, picked up the old iron anklet and ran to his parents. "Look, it must have washed up from a pirate's ship." The child's joy in finding the anklet equaled Cassidy's freedom from being shackled to it.

After an hour of walking and examining rauks along the coastline, Adam leaned against a rauk formation and sighed. "There are just too many rauk formations to decide which one he used on the map. His treasure could be on land or in the sea. We have no resources to look for a treasure in the sea, and I'm sure every experienced treasure hunter in the world has sailed and examined these waters. As for inland, it could be anywhere."

Adam sounded tired and frustrated, and Cassidy felt sorry for him, as she knew he had not slept since being on the plane from Canada, and must be dead on his feet after escaping on the motorbike from Ulf.

"I think we need to find a place to sleep for the night," Cassidy suggested, being exhausted herself from the day's events.

"We can continue this search tomorrow. I slept in the culvert, but you haven't slept for two days. We can come back tomorrow when our minds are fresh and alert...and we need something to eat."

Adam nodded in agreement, and stepped out from between the rauks. Suddenly, he gulped and grabbed Cassidy's arm, pulling her around to the shaded backside of a wide stone column. He quickly pulled his shirt off, much to the shock of Cassidy. "Take your blouse off quick," he ordered and the urgency in his voice made her do so. He tossed their shirts on the ground and kicked them deeper into the shadows. Cassidy stood with arms folded across her brassiere, embarrassed and bewildered.

"They'll recognize our clothes," he whispered, and then pushed her against the rocky wall as far as he could into the shadows. He rested his hands on both sides of her face, his arms shielding her from being recognized. Then he lowered his face to kiss her lips.

Ulf's man, Matts, rounded the corner, looking hastily for Cassidy and Adam. All he noticed was a half-naked young man and girl romancing in the shadows. He disappeared back to Ulf and reported no sign of Cassidy and Adam.

Adam backed away from Cassidy and picked up his T-shirt. "Sorry, but we'd have been dead if he recognized us."

"Aah, you made me hurry so fast, I ripped some buttons off my blouse," Cassidy complained, putting on her blouse and trying to hold the front shut with dignity.

"This is Sweden," Adam said with a calm, straight face.

"Women are known to dress with much less than that on Swedish beaches."

"Well, forget that idea, Mr. Lucino," she said, her face still flushed from the aftermath of his closeness and kiss.

Adam just smiled slightly and peeked around the rauk to carefully check if Ulf and his man were gone. "We better get back to the bike," he suggested. "It's getting late and we have to pick up Mikayla and Mikkel before the Lummelunda caves close for the day. I passed a vacant farmyard back in the lowland when I was trying to get away. It's quite concealed from other buildings, surrounded by hillsides. Nothing around but a herd of goats. I don't think anyone would ever find us there."

Cassidy rested her tired body against a rauk, laden with fossils. She turned her face and came eye-level with a slender fossil in the stone. She slowly raised her hand and let her fingers trace over the spine of a prehistoric marine specimen from long ago. "This fossil resembles a sword or dagger, does it not?" Cassidy shouted to Adam, her heart beginning to race with excitement.

Adam approached her, and leaned in closer to examine the fossil. "Yes, it surely does," he agreed and glanced at her with a fresh sparkle in his eye. "Maybe...Maybe the fossils are the daggers shown on the map."

Cassidy explored around the rauks with quick, eager glances. "Here's another fossil like the one on the first rauk. Maybe they are like stepping stones, leading us on a path to the treasure."

"Wait," Adam halted her search. "It's getting too late. We'll return tomorrow. We have to find safety for the night and get Mikayla and the boy. The fossils aren't going anywhere, and no one knows about their resemblance to daggers except us, so we'll come back."

Adam and Cassidy hurried down the shoreline, and finally reached their bike. "I'll drop you off at that old farm house in the valley, and then fetch Mikayla and the boy back on the bike. We'll have to make a night of it there. Mikayla will likely know where I can shop for some food and water, and gas for the bike. It's getting low on fuel."

At the vacant farmyard, Cassidy dismounted the bike and stood nervously beside Adam as he revved the engine to leave. "Be careful," she said in a feeble voice, afraid that Ulf might intercept him and his sister.

"If I don't return by noon tomorrow, get back to the airport, claim your purse and passport there, and fly back to Canada. You have a return ticket in your purse. Waldo has the Harja file in his collar. Use it as collateral to bribe Ulf into freeing us... if we're still alive. Here's money for a ferry ride back to the mainland, and the key to the rental car to get back to Stockholm. Return the rental car and take a taxi from there to the airport in Arlanda. Here's the list of names that we salvaged from that coffee pot. You can contact Ulf through one of these numbers, once you are safely back in Canada. Tell my father the score. He'll help you."

"Oh, don't even think of such a scenario," Cassidy cried, trying to refuse the money, but he insisted and she took it, knowing he was right to have a backup plan.

"I would give them the Harja file right this minute," Cassidy told him, "if I thought we'd never see or hear from them again, but Mikayla was witness to Simco's murder, so there's no sense in fooling ourselves that they'll ever let us free of this mess alive. They have to get rid of her...and us."

Adam nodded in agreement. Cassidy bravely straightened her body and stepped back from his bike. "Well then, it's getting late. Here's the map to the caves. Stop and buy a blanket for the baby, if you can. It might get chilly here tonight...and cover him with it on the bike. I don't think three are allowed on the bike. You don't want to bring attention to yourselves."

# 13

Cassidy glanced up at the old limestone farm house. The kitchen door swung on one rusty hinge like a fluttering oak leaf. Only half the glass panes were left in the windows and the birds seemed to delight diving in and out the open gaps with precise accuracy. She surmised they had nests everywhere within, and was not wrong, as the floor was littered with bird droppings when she peeked inside.

Cassidy lingered in the doorway, observing the large empty room with a critical eye. She walked back outside, gathered some long grass to form a broom, and tied them onto a stick with her hair band. She swept one large room out as best as she could with the grass broom. She could see the roof on the lean-to bedroom had collapsed, so closed the door and concentrated on trying to make the one large room livable for the night.

There was a hand pump in the yard, so Cassidy gathered an old discarded bucket and tried to pump water. The pump had lost prime from ears of no use, so she retrieved water from a nearby pond, primed the pump and was able to finally draw up water. She smiled at her success, glad that as a child, she had once observed her grandfather prime an old dry pump at a cabin.

She ripped tattered, sun-bleached curtains from the windows to use as scrub rags, and within a few hours, had the floor scrubbed, and the paint-chipped, cupboard shelves and table washed off as best as she could. She tried to keep her mind busy so that she would not imagine horrible things happening to Adam and his sister, not to mention little Mikkel.

Cassidy retrieved a rock from the crumbling foundation outside, and used it to hammer nails back into the hinges on the door. The door would at least prevent animals from wandering in, but she decided not to deny the birds returning to their nests. She had nothing to repair the broken windows with anyway, rain or shine. She was ready for company, and waited patiently to hear the sound of a motorcycle returning, but as dusk settled in, there was only the creaking of the rusty windmill, and night sounds of far off ships.

⌇

*An eye peeped through the wall in the Salter River Mansion, checking out the main entrance room. There had been no sign of life for several days, and so he decided it would be safe to dismount the steps into the lower level of the house to see what had been tampered with. He eyed the obvious searching through the files he had heaped everywhere, and chuckled to himself, as the files had confused many of Ulf's men in the past, who had come in search of the Harja file. He had no idea where Raglan Leslie had hidden the file, and didn't care. It was of little concern to him. He had other scores to settle. It did concern him, however, to find Cassidy Leslie in the house with Adam Lucino. He had worked on a plan for five years, and the two might interfere with that.*

⌇

A stone fireplace stood partly crumbled in a corner of the large room. Cassidy could find no matches to light the fireplace with, and decided the chimney was likely unsafe anyhow, as birds had probably nested in it for years. As nightfall settled in, she longed for a light. Having none, she sat on the doorstep with the moon as her lantern. It was better than sitting in the dark house by herself. At least the moon cast a sparkling, silvery path across the pond nearby.

She thought about Adam's quick decision to embrace and hide her, so that Matts would not recognize them. She wrapped her arms about herself in the cooling air. She knew his actions were merely a distraction to deceive Matts, but it was going to be hard to look at Adam without recalling his kiss.

All seemed peaceful in the deserted farmyard until ghostly figurines suddenly appeared out of the darkness. Cassidy jumped up in such fright that she tumbled down the front steps. She lay at the bottom of the steps, flat on her stomach, half crying and half laughing at herself, as a herd of frightened goats jumped like airborne jackrabbits over her body, and scampered up the hillside. She was sure her heart rate raced for an hour afterward. Adam had better return soon because she didn't think she could stand another scare like that.

It wasn't until near nine o'clock before she heard the welcome sound of a roar approaching closer and closer. Adam's bike puttered up to the doorstep with Mikayla and a blanket-covered Mikkel, who peeked his head out like a gopher, and grinned widely at Cassidy.

"I hide," he said to her, and Cassidy threw her arms around the little boy, and lifted him off the bike.

They carried in armfuls of groceries that were draped over the handlebars of the bike, as well as over Mikayla's arms and around her neck. Mikayla laughed as they tried to unload the groceries off her. "Now I know what a pack horse feels like. We have enough food and water here for a week."

Mikkel held a flashlight while Adam set up a battery operated lantern on the table. Its warm glow brightened the center of the room, and reached out to the corners. "Oh man, this old house looks great," he said to Cassidy. "You did wonders."

"I tried to clean the room a bit with cold water from the well, but cold water with no soap, and a grass broom doesn't do a very good job," Cassidy confessed. "There's an old fireplace in the corner, but I'm not sure how many birds might have built their homes in the chimney over the years, so it may not be safe to light."

"Well, the old iron cook stove looks like it has a simple chimney pipe out the wall, so we'll try that first," Adam suggested with a cheery voice. Mikkel and Adam eagerly went outside in search of some firewood. They returned, opened a lid on the top of the stove, shoved in some wood kindling and lit a match. All stood back, waiting for a plugged chimney to send billows of smoke back into the house, but the ventilation seemed clear, and they let out a successful cheer in unison. "Aah! Now to make coffee," Adam sighed.

Mikayla laughed at her brother, overjoyed at being able to share his presence again. "Yes, and I think the lady who cleaned this house with not a single modern convenience, has earned the first cup of coffee."

"And also this." Adam walked over to Cassidy and withdrew a charm bracelet from his pocket, each charm a figure of the rune alphabet. "I saw it in the store and thought it might be the only runes we ever find." He laughed and clipped the bracelet around her wrist.

Cassidy's mouth opened in surprise and delight. "Oh! What a lovely keepsake. How thoughtful!" She eyed him for a quiet moment and then moved in closer and kissed his lips softly. Perhaps such a sweet kiss held more passion than the wildest of kisses, and it rendered Adam speechless and somewhat shy in front of his sister.

Silence hung in the air, as if no one wanted to destroy the captivating moment. Then suddenly Mikkel's little voice spoke up timidly, "Are we going to have supper tonight?"

An explosion of laughter burst from all the adults, as they raced to unload the groceries and make a feast of bread, fruit, roast lamb and jam.

Mikkel fell asleep, tucked in several blankets close to the cook stove for warmth, while Adam seated himself beside his sister on the floor. "Do you know anything, Mickie, that might help us get out of this mess alive?"

Mikayla sighed deeply. "If I knew how to get Mikkel to a safe place, I would have done it years ago, but Mikkel doesn't even have a passport. I have no way to get him out of the country, and I won't risk his life trying. Ulf is still legally his father. Right now, he could have me arrested for kidnapping, and be granted full custody of the boy. Until we prove Ulf a criminal, I am more of a criminal in the eyes of the law than he is."

Cassidy spoke softly so as not to waken Mikkel. "I think you had better remain hidden. Perhaps Adam and I should go back to the beach tomorrow to scout around and see if we can figure out any clues to the treasure. Ulf will never stop hunting us until we come up with an answer. If we have to trade the treasure's whereabouts for our lives, we will."

Cassidy stood up and moved her blanket closer to Adam. "You and Mikkel have enough food and water to last a few days here. Just don't light the stove in the daytime for fear someone sees the smoke. Only a herd of goats seem to hang out here, so I think you will be safe."

"Ulf will be looking mainly for you and Adam," Mikayla replied. "He will be angry at my escape, but I will not be his top priority. The Harja file is more valuable to him than anything. He has my passport, so knows I cannot escape from Sweden without first getting it out of his vault. He'll plan to take care of me later. You will be the center of his attention right now."

With that, they wrapped blankets about themselves, and tried to find comfort on the hard, wooden floor. Cassidy wiggled closer to Adam and rested her head on his stomach for a pillow. "Waldo made a better pillow, but you'll do," she kidded.

"Waldo!" Adam smiled at the thought of his buddy. "I miss that dog." He yawned from exhaustion and fell asleep within minutes, not having time to miss the comfort of a pillow beneath his head.

# 14

It was dusk, so no curious eyes could comprehend what was going on outside the Salter River Mansion. A truck backed up close to the front veranda steps, and after a few moments, a thin man loaded box after box of files into the back of the truck. When done, he drove away, aimed for a recycling bin where he could dispose of the boxes. There was no fear of anyone reading the files, as they were a bunch of useless chatter on paper, created only to entice Ulf back to Canada. Unfortunately, Ulf had previously sent only his men to search for the Harja File. A second plan was needed to coax Ulf to Canada.

It appeared to the man that Cassidy and Adam had discovered the file. If such was the case, then Ulf would have no reason to return to Canada in search of it. He would be too busy chasing the young couple all over Gotland Island. He had to somehow convince Ulf that Cassidy and Adam only had a decoy, and that he had the real file. The wheels began clicking in his head and he smiled to himself. One might as well have a little fun in catching a killer. It needn't be all stress.

❧

Cassidy and Adam walked beside their bike for a long

distance before starting up the motor to drive to the rauks. They wanted no one to report any suspicious action coming from the vacant farmyard. Mikayla had agreed to stay hidden at the farmyard with her son until Adam and Cassidy figured out a plan for their escape to safety.

Once close to the rauks, Cassidy and Adam concealed their motorbike amongst the rocks a short distance from the shoreline. They now examined the unique and fascinating sea stacks, searching for more marine fossils that resembled daggers. Some rauks held multi fossils, which began to discourage their theory on whether the fossils were relevant to the treasure or not.

"There's too many fossils the same," Cassidy sighed. "Maybe they don't represent daggers at all."

Adam recalled what was on the map. "It showed three daggers, one on top of the other. Perhaps we need to look for a set of three fossils, not singles."

Like panhandlers searching for gold, Cassidy and Adam scoured the rauks, looking for dagger-like fossils that matched the symbols on the map. They were so engrossed in their hunt that they did not notice Ulf Lindberg with Matts slinking snakelike from rauk to rauk, slowly working their way closer to where the young couple examined the rock formations.

As Mikayla feared, acquaintances of Ulf's, had recognized his wife near the rauks the day before, walking and talking at length with strangers, and had mentioned it to Ulf. It did not take Ulf long to hit for the shoreline, strung with sculptured rock formations that lined the beach like sentries.

Suddenly, Matts stumbled and fell partly into the open, his presence instantly revealed to Adam and Cassidy. Adam jerked his head around at the sound, noticed Matts with a revolver in his hand, and yelled to Cassidy in a frantic voice. "Run to the bike, Cass. Don't look back. Just run."

Two shots rang out. One bullet buzzed past Adam's ear, and the other caught him in his side. Adam fell, and then quickly gathered himself to his feet and continued running to where they had hidden the motorbike. Cassidy ran for her life in front of him, not realizing that Adam had been wounded.

Adam left a trail of blood in the sand, which encouraged Ulf to attack even more intensely. Adam could hear Ulf shouting to Matts, "Kill him. We don't need him. She'll spill where it's hidden. Shoot him! Shoot him!" Another bullet spit dust at his feet as he reached the motorbike, swung a leg over and torpedoed away with Cassidy riding on the seat behind him. They cut across fields, rough terrain and along tree lines where they were less noticeable, searching for a place safe enough to hide. Finally, Adam was too weak to handle the bike, and he slowed to a stop.

Cassidy had held her arms tightly around his waist to prevent herself from falling off. Now, as they halted in a treed meadow, she dismounted the bike and withdrew her hands from around his waist. Suddenly, she realized her hands were covered in blood, and she looked up to see Adam sink to his knees.

"Oh Adam! You're shot," she cried in shock and anguish, and laid him on his back in the grass. She began ripping her blouse in strips and held them tight over his wound to try and stop the bleeding. She took both his hands and put them over the wound. "Press hard," she implored desperately. "We have to stop the bleeding, or you'll bleed to death." She rolled him slightly over to his side to check his back. "The bullet has gone clean through, so we have two holes to stop bleeding from." She removed his jacket and shirt, and began tearing his shirt into strips to wrap around his torso to hold the compresses on tightly.

Adam looked at her weakly. He had already lost a lot of blood while traveling, and felt unable to focus clearly on her face. "Can you ride the bike? You have to get out of here before they find us."

"I'm not leaving you, Adam. I got you into this mess." She looked around the meadow in despair. She was well aware that he could bleed to death, and that she had to react quickly. Suddenly, she thought of his cell phone in his backpack and ran to the bike to retrieve it. The battery in her own phone was dead, but she prayed Adam's phone still had power.

"I sup..pose this will be a great adventure...to tell our children someday," Adam murmured with a moan, struggling to control pain as he spoke.

Cassidy gave a short little laugh, and reached a hand over to ruffle his hair. "Yes, and I can just imagine them all sitting around a campfire listening to the story...and each of them having your wild crazy hair."

"And... they'll all be ...," Adam coughed and his voice slowly faded, "be...be hockey players."

"Then it's a good thing I'm a dentist," she joked through tearful eyes, but she didn't think Adam heard, as his eyes were closed.

Cassidy turned her attention to the cell phone. She knew the batteries may be low, and that it was a slim chance for her to be able to reach her father stationed in the Middle East, but she had to try. By telling his superiors that it was a case of life or death, hopefully, her father could be contacted.

It took several exchanges of contacts, and speaking to a Captain well acquainted with Cassidy's father, to finally get her father on the phone. "Oh Daddy," Cassidy broke down in tearful relief. "I can't talk long because the phone battery might die. Please listen carefully. I'm on Gotland Island. I'm in real bad trouble. A man called Ulf Lindberg threatened my life if I did not give him a treasure map called the Harja file. I don't know if you know anything about it or not, but Uncle Raglan had the map hidden in his house. I'm with Adam Lucino. They've shot him and we're somewhere inland from the northern coastline where the rauks are. I don't know where to take him. He'll bleed to death if I don't get him help soon. I don't know who to trust, Daddy...or where to go."

"Land sakes, sweetheart. What have you got yourself into? Well, we'll talk about that later. I have a doctor friend in Visby. You can trust him with your life. I'll arrange for him to meet you north of Visby on a sharp bend in the road near a tall bridge. Dr. Neilsson will be waiting. What are you driving, honey?"

"Just a motorcycle. I've got to go. Every minute counts. I love you. Bye."

Cassidy cut more strips of cloth and used jacket sleeves to join all together to make a long, strong scarf. With Adam's help, she struggled to sit him upright on the bike. Cassidy wrapped the long scarf of cloth behind his back and then mounted in front of him. She picked up both ends of the scarf and tied them about her middle, drawing Adam up close to her back for support. She hoped the scarf would keep him tight against her and prevent him from falling off. She then tied his wrists in front of her for added stability and inhaled a long, brave breath.

Cassidy was not experienced at riding a motorbike, but she had driven three- wheelers and quads at her friend's place back home, so decided if she traveled slowly at first, that she would get the hang of it by the time she reached the highway. The main thing was not to tip over and cause a disaster with Adam tied to her back. She revved the engine as she had seen Adam do. Then she opened the throttle bit by bit, and took her foot off the clutch slowly, so as not to take off like a rocket. She moved slowly at first in short, jerky motions, but gradually as she gained confidence and better balance on the bike, her speed increased on the way back to Visby.

# 15

As Cassidy traveled down the road on the motorcycle, her eyes darted in all directions for fear of running into Ulf's gang. She yelled back to Adam. "I can hear your breathing, Adam. If it stops, I swear I'll kill you."

Adam didn't answer, as he had passed into unconsciousness from lack of blood, and was like a rag doll attached to her back. Cassidy could feel his warmth against her back, head flush against her neck, and prayed she would reach the doctor fast.

Finally, Cassidy roared up to bridge at a sharp bend in the road where an ambulance was parked on the shoulder of the road. A figure in a doctor's white smock stepped out of the vehicle and walked quickly towards her. He shouted, "I'm Dr. Neilsson." He was younger than she had imagined, perhaps in his mid-forties, and her knees shook with fear that he may not be the man her father sent to help them.

Dr. Neilsson had brought along a trusted ambulance driver, and they helped Cassidy untie the support scarves from around her waist, and lower Adam carefully onto a stretcher. He bent over Adam, took his pulse, and checked his wounds. Then he turned to Cassidy. "He's lost a lot of blood. I'll radio ahead to prepare the hospital for his arrival."

They quickly discarded the motorbike behind a clump of brushes and hit for the hospital. On the way, Cassidy explained part of her unbelievable tale to Dr. Neilsson. The doctor assured her that the Gotland police would station guards outside Adam's hospital door, but Cassidy was nervous to leave Adam's side. Perhaps Ulf had connections in the police force. It was hard to trust anyone in a strange land. Finally, she had no choice but to leave Adam in the hospital, and ask Dr. Neilsson if she could borrow his personal car to return to the vacant farm house and rescue Mikayla and Mikkel.

Dr. Neilsson insisted on accompanying her. "Your friend has lost a lot of blood, but he'll be okay. The bullet fortunately missed his organs. We'll let him sleep and rest a bit while we pick up his sister and nephew. Don't worry! The police will guard him. His sister and child can stay at my place. No one would think to look for them there. First, we'll get you a change of clothing and a shower, as you're covered in blood. We don't want you scaring half my patients." He instructed some nurses to bring her a pair of pajamas and robe, and directed her to a shower.

Once showered and dressed in clean hospital attire, Cassidy followed Dr. Neilsson out to his car. She looked like a runaway hospital patient, but had no other clothes to wear.

When Mikayla saw a strange, blue vehicle drive around the corner, she panicked and squeezed out a back window with her son. She hid with Mikkel in a tumbled down goat shed, peeping through the cracks to see who had approached the farmyard. Mikkel clung desperately to his mother's leg, sensing her fear. She bent over and pressed a finger to her lips to indicate to Mikkel that he must be quiet. A trembling Mikkel buried his face in his mother's pant leg and remained quiet as a mouse.

Cassidy called and called until finally, Mikayla recognized Cassidy in the hospital robe. Gingerly, she stepped out of the shed with her son behind her, not completely confident that the situation was safe, but trusting Cassidy would never put Mikkel in danger. Mikayla then noticed Adam was not with Cassidy, and her eyes grew large with fear.

"Adam is alright," Cassidy quickly assured her. "This is Dr. Neilsson, a friend of my father's." Cassidy proceeded to explain what had happened with the shooting. Mikayla was overwhelmed with shock and concern for her brother, and began to sob. After further reassurance that Adam would be fine, Mikayla regained composure, and they transferred their few belongings from the old house into the doctor's car.

"Seeing as you will be staying at my house, "Dr. Neilsson spoke gently to Mikayla, "you can call me Daniel. It will be nice to have some human company instead of that spoiled cat of mine."

Mikkel's little eyes sparkled with interest, as Ulf had never allowed him a pet of any kind. Ulf grouped puppies and kittens in with children; nothing but mouths to feed and objects to trip over.

"You have a cat?" Mikkel asked with enthusiasm, hopeful that he might be able to pet and feed the animal.

Dr. Daniel Neilsson swung Mikkel up onto shoulders and carried him out to the car while spinning stories about his cat. The four year old was instantly hypnotized by the young doctor's tales, and forgot his fear of previously hiding in the goat shed.

"Do you know that silly cat likes vegetables?" Dr. Neilsson complained, shaking his head in dismay. "Now isn't a cat supposed to chase mice? Not Nikolass. He likes yams and carrots."

Mikayla and Cassidy could hear Mikkel's childish giggles from across the yard. "He has a good way with children," Cassidy observed aloud, but Mikayla's face expressed only signs of anxiety. Ulf had threatened Mikkel's life many times if she tried to contact her family. It was hard for her to suddenly trust a stranger with her son.

Cassidy noticed Mikayla's vigilant eyes following the doctor. She understood the woman's concern for her child, and rested a calming hand upon her shoulder. "He's a friend of my father's. Don't worry, Mikayla. My father is a good judge of character."

Mikayla smiled at Cassidy, and tried to let her shoulders relax, but she did not take her eyes off Mikkel.

Once the doctor settled Mikayla and Mikkel into his house, he returned to the hospital with Cassidy. The hospital staff had kindly washed and dried Cassidy's clothing while she was gone, and now returned them to her. She gratefully changed out of her hospital attire, and then sat and watched Adam sleep until the police came to take her down to the station for statements.

She revealed all she knew to the police except details on the Harja file's treasure map. Such information, she kept to herself. The police were not concerned about treasure, as treasure hunts were common on Gotland Island. Just about every tourist had their eyes glued to the ground, hoping to kick up an ancient coin. What the police wanted was criminal evidence against Ulf Lindberg, whom they knew to deal in selling stolen merchandise to shady collectors.

Cassidy returned to the hospital somewhat downhearted from the police station. Her frustration bubbled over when Dr. Neilsson entered the hospital room to check on Adam.

"There's no witness to who fired and shot Adam," Cassidy's voice trembled in defeat. "Adam heard Ulf order Matts to shoot, but he didn't see him pull the trigger." She ran agitated fingers through her hair. "Mikayla witnessed a taxi driver get murdered back in Canada five years ago, but he's floating in the Great Lakes. Without a body, no one can prove Ulf murdered anybody...Mikayla can claim she was kidnapped, but they are legally married and even have a child together, so in the eyes of the law, it would not appear she was kidnapped. Ulf will just counteract, and say their marriage wasn't going well and now she's telling false tales to discredit him, so she can gain custody of the child." She threw her hands up in despair. "How do we stop this man from killing us all?"

Dr. Neilsson put a comforting hand upon her shoulder. "You're exhausted, young lady. Best you go back to my house and get a good night's sleep. Mikayla and the boy are in the spare room. There's a sofa-bed in the living room, and blankets in a closet in the hallway. Help yourself to the fridge. If you don't get some rest, this young fellow is going to be wide awake tomorrow morning, and you'll be a zombie. Off you go. Take my car. I'll catch a taxi later." He handed his keys to her and she dragged her feet out of the hospital.

Cassidy longed to call her mother and let her know she was okay, but she could not risk Ulf tracing the phone back to Dr. Neilsson's residence, or finding Adam in the hospital. She had spoken to her father from the police station and he said he would explain the situation to her mother, so that was the best she could do until Adam was well enough to leave the hospital.

∾⌒∾

*He unlocked the attic door and made his way down to the ground floor without the usual caution. He stretched his arms and looked about the place. It was much neater now that he had taken all the files away. He made himself a pot of coffee. He recalled the list of phone numbers that Raglan had left Cassidy in the coffee pot. He was glad he wrote the numbers down for himself. Hopefully, the numbers would allow him to communicate with Ulf, and set his plan in motion. He withdrew an electronic device from his pocket and pressed a button. Instantly a hair-raising wolf howl chilled the air. Man! He loved that sound!*

∾⌒∾

Ulf picked up his phone and heard Henrik practically screaming on the other end of the line. "Hold it! Hold it!" Ulf bellowed back. "What do you mean the file is back at Raglan

Leslie's? Get over here now."

In a matter of minutes, Lars and Henrik stampeded through the door. Henrik was animated about the file. "Someone called one of the contact numbers we gave to Raglan Leslie," he explained hastily between gulps of gasping breaths. "The man insisted he had the file and that he had placed a decoy for Miss Leslie to discover, knowing she would follow false clues to Gotland Island and give him free reign to bargain with you."

Ulf rubbed his chin thoughtfully, and walked about the room to savor the news. He dragged a finger along the mantel piece, as if looking for a trace of dust. "He's taken a long time to come forward. Did he mention Mikayla or the boy?"

Henrik spoke cautiously so as not to upset Ulf. "Not a word about your wife and child, sir... Sorry about them leaving you, sir."

Ulf whirled about, his eyes inflamed with anger. "Don't coddle me, Henrik. You know the score. She was no more of a wife to me than a fake laugh on a clown...and that kid...he was just a tape across her mouth. Nothing more." He turned back to look out the window, arms folded tightly across his chest. "The only reason I'm asking about her is she might have something to do with the file being back at Raglan's. I always figured she was hiding something. What else did he say?"

"That he wanted to meet with you...midnight at the Salter River Mansion in four days' time," Lars replied. "Bring twenty million and he'll give you the file...and you have to come in person."

"He wants twenty million! The bloodsucker! What proof did he give you that he has the file?" Ulf paced back and forth across the room with discontent. "Surely, he doesn't expect us to turn over twenty million dollars without proof of him having the file."

"He said to tell you he has four more coins from Skully's treasure, same identifying pecking marks, and that you will know if they are genuine when you see them, seeing as you are an expert on the matter. He will tell you where he found them, give you the coins, plus the real Harja treasure map…for the price of twenty million."

Ulf stopped pacing and his sunken shoulders squared and uplifted with power once more. "When I saw Mikayla's coin, I knew it came from Skully's plunder." Ulf was pumped to think he had been right about the treasure. "Raglan had the map all this time and he knew where the treasure was hidden. Four more coins! It's there, boys! I had a feeling that old fox was lying to me about not knowing where his wife hid the Harja file…He had some bloody nerve to up and die on me."

"Why wouldn't Raglan grab the treasure and reap the profit himself?" Lars asked. "The runic dagger is worth more than the treasure to a lot of people. Why hide it and keep the fact a secret all these years?"

Ulf smiled deviously. "Because he was an honest man. He would do nothing until he located the treasure for sure…and if true, the fool would most likely hand it over to some musty old museum."

Ulf opened a cabinet and withdrew a bottle of wine. "Now

me, I don't claim to be an honorable man. No, I am 100% a thieving scoundrel." His men nodded in agreement. "If we find treasure," Ulf continued, "we cannot just pick up our trunk of coins and jewels and sail off to live in luxury the rest of our lives. You can't exactly buy a yacht with medieval coins. There are laws and historical claims and government rights and land rights and regulations to such finds. I simply like to avoid such nuisances."

Ulf filled four glasses with expensive wine, and handed them to his men. "I could sell the location of the treasure rather than recover it, and take a chance on getting only a small piece of the pie...or I could dispose of obstacles in my way and bathe in millions. Simple choice!" He held his own glass up in a toast to himself, while his men smiled in amusement. "To me," Ulf said.

Lars intervened in Ulf's rationality. "The only problem now, Boss, is that Raglan Leslie was soft, and would have eventually given up the Harja file in exchange for your Missus and the boy, but now, someone else is involved and he wants money for the file and doesn't appear to have any problem dealing with...dogs."

This time, it was Ulf who laughed, and slapped Lars on the back with a playful cuff. "Then, us dogs best hurry and make flight arrangements to Canada. This fellow sounds dirty enough to be one of us."

# 16

As soon as the Gotland police discovered that Ulf and his men had left for Canada, they informed Adam and Cassidy of their escape. Adam did not hesitate to call his father and reveal the whole unbelievable tale to them, including news that their daughter was alive and well with a four year old son by her kidnapper. His parents were thrilled to know Mikayla was alive, despite the frightening circumstances, and insisted on booking the first available plane to Sweden to reunite with her and Mikkel.

Adam quickly arranged for his uncle, Georgio Lucino to take Waldo and the cat and leave no one at the Lucino residence for Ulf to get his hands on. Cassidy's father, likewise, sent her mother to her sister's residence in Alberta, leaving not a soul for Ulf to contact or harm when he arrived.

Cassidy and Adam did not know that a third party, the attic dweller in the Salter River Mansion, was whom Ulf Lindberg planned to deal with upon arriving in Canada, and Ulf had no idea that he was about to deal with a ghost.

Dr. Neisson made it clear to Adam that he should not be scouring the rauks along the Baltic Sea in his condition, for fear of his wounds reopening. He advised Adam to relax quietly in the hospital for a few more days, and then take things easy for a while. His caution fell on deaf ears. With the knowledge that Ulf and his men were far away in Canada, Adam felt now was the safest opportunity to search out fossil clues in the rauks. Mikayla suggested he stay back and babysit Mikkel while she accompany Cassidy to the rauks, but Adam convinced his sister that she was easily recognizable to Ulf's contacts, and needed to remain hidden, especially since she was the only witness to Ulf murdering Simco.

The young doctor offered his car for Cassidy and Adam to use in returning to the Baltic Sea, instead of taking the old motorcycle. Adam needed as little rough movement as possible. They also needed to remain inconspicuous, for although Ulf had taken his top men to Canada with him, they feared others were likely on Ulf's payroll.

Cassidy and Adam parked the vehicle in a parking lot near the Baltic Sea and strolled slowly towards the rauks. They sat down in the first rauk's shade to rest awhile before continuing on. Adam leaned his head back on the limestone formation and closed his eyes. Cassidy nonchalantly traced patterns in the sand with the tip of her finger, giving Adam time to rest. When she looked up, she noticed Adam had fallen fast asleep. She didn't have the heart to waken him, for she knew he was still weak from being shot and needed the rest. She slipped a note in his hand, saying she would return shortly, and let him sleep at the base of the rauk while she checked further by herself.

After half an hour, Cassidy returned to check on Adam, but he was gone. Her heart began to race. Had Ulf's men kidnapped him? She knew he could not have come her direction or she would have met him on her return, and he had no reason to return to the car, unless he was in need of a doctor. Wild thoughts of him captured or seriously bleeding spun in her head. She checked the ground surrounding the rauk, but the soil showed no trace of a struggle or bleeding. She tried to convince herself that there would be too many witnesses to foul play, as other tourists were about. When she reached the car and opened the door, a note was waiting for her on the front seat.

*"Keep looking for dagger formations in the rauks. I have gone to Canada. Hitched a ride with a fellow tourist to the ferry. I'll return the rental car on my way to airport. Don't follow me. I have a plan. Our folks are safe, so stay with Mikayla. Don't worry. You know I would never do anything foolish. -- Adam"*

Cassidy knew Adam was quite capable of doing something foolish, and her stomach felt sick. Taking off alone in his condition was a very foolish idea. She sat in the car for a few minutes, trying to decide whether she had enough time to intercept him at the ferry before he had chance to cross to the mainland. Adam was in no condition to be off on his own, doing goodness knows what. She still had her passport and baggage to claim at the Arlanda airport, but first she must return the car to Dr. Neilsson's residence and explain Adam's note to Daniel and Mikayla.

Daniel planned to take Mikayla and Mikkel to the Arlanda airport the following morning to meet her parents, so he convinced Cassidy to wait and accompany them. Then he could vouch for her identity and help her retrieve her belongings from security at the airport. Surely Adam would not get into trouble in that short time.

Mikayla could sense Cassidy's concern for Adam, and reassured her, "Don't worry about Adam. He'll be careful. He was never one to take foolish chances."

Apprehension splashed clearly across Cassidy's face. "Somehow, I picture Adam jumping from one roof-top to another with a gun in one hand and a stick of dynamite in the other."

Mikayla burst into laughter. She remembered a young shy brother from years ago. "I think you've been watching too many detective movies. Adam is a quiet, resigned kind of guy, not the sort to be setting off dynamite sticks under bridges."

Cassidy smiled back, but deep inside her gut, she knew she better get to Canada before Adam got himself killed. Brave hearts rarely wear their capabilities on their sleeves. They sit back in the shadows, often underestimated until needed. Then they step out and save the day. That was Adam Lucino. She had once underestimated him, but never again.

Cassidy savored the reunion between Mikayla and her Lucino parents before she left on her flight back to Canada. She would tell Adam all about the joyous hugs and tears, and the look on Mikkel's face when his grandparents handed him a fluffy Polar Bear toy almost as big as he was. Her and Daniel stood back quietly and drank in the emotional meeting of the Lucino parents with their daughter. There would be time enough later for her parents to learn about Mikayla's years of fear for herself and her son. For now, there was only joy and gratitude for her safe return.

Upon landing in Canada, Cassidy immediately purchased a wig to disguise her appearance, and took a taxi to a hotel. She dared not return to the Salter River mansion in case Ulf was in the vicinity. She had no key to enter Adam's residence, so hoped her and Adam's paths would soon cross. Cassidy took a taxi close to the mansion property, and then walked on foot to the rest of her destination.

A granite wall loomed up behind the Salter River mansion, its rocky shelf level with the second story roof top. A hiking trail wound along the edge of the cliff with only a simple warning, "Cliff edges may crumble. Keep to Walking Trail."

From this majestic view point, Cassidy could survey the scene below. There appeared to be no movement in the yard, but that didn't mean Ulf was not inside, or if not inside, possibly watching from some other vantage point. There had to be a reason why Ulf suddenly left Sweden for Canada, and Cassidy was positive that sooner or later, he would return to the mansion.

Cassidy brought a warm, dark colored blanket to throw about her shoulders for when the evening air cooled. She wanted no bright clothing to highlight her against the natural backdrop of trees and cliff formations. Things happen when darkness closes in, and Cassidy wanted to be present for whatever action might take place. She brought binoculars, but dusk increasingly made it difficult to use them. Still, she waited...and waited. She was grateful for a clear sky and three-quarter moon, which at least, allowed some definition of the yard. She would be able to see if a person walked about the yard, and that was all she was hoping for.

The crack of twigs behind Cassidy startled her into almost falling off the cliff edge. White tailed deer escaped down the trail at the sight of a human being, and she heaved a sigh of relief, thankful it had not been one of Ulf's men. One little push from anyone would have sent her to her death over the cliff face.

About ten o'clock in the evening, the thin form of a man emerged from behind a tall stone wall to the one side of the mansion, and quickly entered the rear of the building through a small exit door. Cassidy knew the door was connected to a small pantry where canned preserves, flour, sugar and other cooking supplies had once been stored.

Cassidy could not recognize the thin man in the dim moonlight, but she knew by his physique that the figure was not Adam, Ulf, or any of Ulf's men that she had met. She gave the figure ample time to enter and leave the pantry room before she crept down the cliff side, and approached the back of the house. She noted a small high window and decided to try and enter through it, as the exit door was locked.

Cassidy needed something to stand on to hoist herself up high enough to push the window up, so she could climb in. She looked about and saw an old rain barrel at the corner of the house, and rolled it beneath the pantry window. She grabbed the window sill with both hands and went to hoist her legs up on the barrel when two hands suddenly encircled her body from behind, one hand about her waist and the other over her mouth so she could not scream.

Cassidy kicked back with all the force she could muster and nailed the abductor square in the shins with her hard boot heel. He freed her with a muffled yelp, and she turned to find Adam bending over, holding his leg in agonizing pain. He looked up at her, squinting in agony. "Geez!" he moaned in a half whisper. "You could have at least kicked my good leg."

Cassidy whispered back in frustration, yanking her blond wig off her head. "Well, how in heavens did you expect me to know it was you in the dark - grabbing me from behind like that? I nearly fainted."

"I doubt you would ever faint," Adam grated back, still rubbing his injured leg.

# 17

Cassidy whispered, "I saw a thin man enter a short time ago. There's a small pantry on the other side, which is seldom used. I thought I would sneak in, and listen to any conversations that might take place. I'm sure Ulf and his men will come here, as this is the only place that has any connection to the Harja file. What have you found out...and how are you feeling? You shouldn't have taken off alone in your condition. You have a bullet hole clean through you."

Adam kept his voice low so no one would hear them talking. "I'm okay. Sore as can be, but okay. I haven't seen any of Ulf's bunch yet, but they'll be planning something. I've mostly been hiding in the bush. Didn't recognize you at first with your long blond hair, but I figured no other girl would be climbing in the window at this time of night." He surveyed the window for a moment. "Well, let's get you through the window without making any noise. Good thing you didn't step up on the barrel. The rotten wood slats in that old thing would have splattered like a pumpkin, and woke the whole neighborhood."

"You mustn't lift in your condition," Cassidy said. "Just steady me while I jump high enough to grab the window sill. Then I think I can pull myself up." Adam knelt down on one knee and told her to use his good knee as a stool to hoist herself up on. She did so and slid the window open. She cautiously opened the pantry door to allow Adam entry, then locked it from the inside, so no one would notice any change in the room.

The couple removed their shoes, so not even the slightest tap of a shoe on the hardwood floors would reach keen ears. Cassidy hid their shoes behind an old butter churn in the pantry and then, as she knew the layout of the house, beckoned Adam to follow her down the dark hallway.

The hallway led to the large open room at the entrance of the house. This was where Raglan Leslie spent most of his later years, not bothering with the upper floors of the sprawling mansion. The north side of the large open room supported a small kitchenette with cupboards, sink, stove and refrigerator. On the opposite side, loomed a huge stone fireplace that warmed most of the bottom floor of the house in bygone times. A large sofa separated the fireplace from the kitchenette and faced the grand front entrance, awaiting Ulf's arrival. To the east, a spacious, winding staircase faded into the shadows, the edges of each vanishing step painted by the glow of the fireplace.

They sat anxiously on a long bench in the hallway beneath a row of pegs where visitors once hung their coats and hats. Cassidy slightly opened the door to peek into the large entrance room. A sliver of light from the glowing fireplace painted a luminous strip down the center of Cassidy's face. She glanced up and smiled to see one of Raglan's old caps still hanging on a peg above her head. She retrieved it, and slapped it on her head. Adam didn't say anything. He had grown to expect strange actions from Cassidy Leslie. For Cassidy, she thought her uncle would like to be in on this adventure.

It was nearing midnight and Cassidy's legs began to fidget

with having to sit still for so long. The fireplace coated a faint golden lacquer across the room's fixtures, so only slight forms of furniture could be distinguished. Suddenly, several candles sprung to life with an eerie flame, as if waiting for the stroke of midnight from the old grandfather clock in the corner.

Cassidy shivered as the mellow candle light brightened the opening her and Adam were peering through. She pulled slightly back into the shadows. Only her two eyes now reflected the candle light. She had seen no one light the candles. They had mysteriously burst into flame by themselves. She swore she could hear her heart pounding in her chest and hoped no one else would hear it.

As the clock chimed midnight, a solid knock rapped on the door. Simultaneously, a spine-tingling wolf howl chilled every living creature within a mile. Ulf opened the door, followed by Henrik, and laughed as he crossed the threshold. "Oh, that was a good one. Poor Henrik near pissed his pants, but I dare say I have faced more fearsome welcomes in my lifetime than a wolf howl."

"So have I," a deep voice spoke from the shadows, but Cassidy could see no person connected to the voice. "Help yourselves to a drink, me hearties," the voice invited, sounding very much like a pirate. The table displayed several glasses and a bottle of expensive wine. Henrik did not hesitate to accept the offer. Ulf was more cautious and waited to see if Henrik was poisoned and rolling on the floor before taking a sip himself.

Ulf sat his glass down and spoke into the shadows. "Show yourself. I do not deal with someone who won't face me. Makes me think you are a dishonest man."

"You have twenty million?" the voice inquired, this time from the opposite side of the room.

Ulf whirled about to face the mysterious voice. "Do you think I am fool enough to walk through your front door with twenty million? First, I need proof that you have the Harja file."

"Fair enough!" the voice complied. "And I be needing proof of Mikayla and her son's freedom." This time the voice appeared to come from the ceiling.

The moving voice antagonized Ulf and he spoke sharply in reply, "The bargain was twenty million for the Harja file. Nothing in the bargain that included the Lucino woman and her brat. Besides, unfortunately for her, she knows too much, and I can't have that."

Cassidy could see Adam's fists clench at the mention of Mikayla. Knowing what Ulf had done to his sister for five years and that Ulf planned to dispose of her, made it difficult for Adam to keep his temper bottled.

Now the voice floated down from the upper staircase. "No Mikayla and Mikkel. No Harja File."

The veins in Ulf's neck began to bulge with a rise in his temperament. He contemplated for a few minutes and then conferred with Henrik. After a couple seconds, he demanded firmly, "Unless you show yourself, the deal is off."

"But I can't," the traveling voice echoed from above Cassidy and Adam's heads in the hallway. Cassidy's eyes bulged with fear that Ulf would rip the door open to the hallway, and discover the two of them sitting like vulnerable ducks in open water. They both realized that someone had wired the house with a sound system, which could be triggered from numerous locations.

.

"I'm dead," the voice continued with a chilling laugh. "But death has benefits. As a ghost, I know all yer secrets."

"Who cares?" Ulf roared, and slammed his fist on the table, causing the wine bottle to teeter before Henrik grabbed and steadied the precious potion. "I've come a long way and sacrificed a hunt to deal with you. You either slap that Harja file on this table in five seconds or I'll machine-gun this place to hell, and I swear one of the bullets will find you by the time Henrik is done."

Adam grabbed Cassidy's arm to pull her away from their location, signaling for them to get out of the hallway in case Henrik started shelling the place. Cassidy hesitated for a moment, not wanting to miss the next consultation between Ulf and the ghost.

"You already killed me once," the ghost's voice echoed about the room. "You can't do it again. I be now in Lake Superior with your bullet in me brain."

"Ulf hesitated and then spoke with a suspicious half whisper. "Simco?"

For a few minutes, all remained quiet as a tomb. All that moved was the eyeballs of the two men circling the room, searching for a body to go with the mysterious voice. Henrik's fingers folded tightly around the trigger of his weapon as he backed slowly towards the front entrance with Ulf.

"Now, are yeh saying you shot poor old Simco?" the voice asked, trying to get an affirmative confession out of Ulf.

Ulf yanked the front door open, frustrated and angry that his plan for a simple trade was not going smoothly. "Yes, I shot you, you worthless old coot, and I'm sorely disappointed to find you're not at the bottom of Lake Superior. But if you think you can trick me into giving up twenty million for the sole witness to that insignificant incident, well, think again…Now unless you hand over the Harja file, I will drive away with my twenty million, but first, Henrik will shell this place so there's not even two boards to lean together. In which case, you will be sawdust floating across the river".

The room was silent, so Ulf continued with his threat. "Then I just might go dangle Mikayla's kid over a bridge until she reveals where the Harja file is…and if my wife doesn't know, which is what she's been saying for the past five years, well, guess it's time to end our marriage with a double splash."

With that, Ulf and Henrik retreated out the door and hurried towards their rented van where they expected to find Lars guarding a suitcase containing twenty million dollars. Once at the van, Ulf glanced at Henrik with a shocked look on his face. Lars and the money were gone, and the sound of police sirens were filling the air, louder than a stadium after a hometown win.

# 18

Within seconds, three quarters of the Salter River police force poured into the yard and surrounded Ulf and Henrik. The Police Captain walked out of the house with an elderly man of African descent, and announced, "Ulf Lindberg, you are charged with the attempted murders of Simon Cobalt and Adam Lucino, the kidnapping of Mikayla Lucino and death threats against her and her son. Henrik Bjorn, you are charged with aiding and abetting a known criminal and possession of an illegal firearm. The Captain then listened to a fellow officer read Ulf and Henrik their full legal rights, and watched as they were handcuffed and taken away.

Simco was much relieved to see Cassidy and Adam safe, and know Mikayla and her son were rescued. He explained, "Your uncle hid me in the attic after I swam out of that freezin' lake. I wandered half dazed down the shores of Salter River until I reached the mansion, bleeding half to death with a head wound. I crawled to his door like a wet lizard. Raglan was used to nursin' soldiers in the army, so he fixed me up real good. We decided to keep me dead to Ulf until we could trick the devil into admitting he tried to kill me. But that idea took a lotta years. Couldn't risk Mikayla's life, and then the child was born. Couldn't do a single hoot except stall Ulf over the Harja file, hoping to get her away from him somehow."

Simco sighed with relief. "Finally, today the Police Chief

witnessed Ulf admit to trying to murder me, and threatening Mikayla and her son. I hope they put him away for a long time."

"Uncle Raglan would be so proud of you," Cassidy praised, giving the old man a huge hug. "That was really a clever idea with the moving voices. It completely unnerved Ulf until he lost composure and talked himself into admittance."

Simco motioned back towards the table in the entrance room. "I put your uncle's favorite wine on the table. Thought Raglan would get a kick out of that. When he got feeling poorly and moved to the care home, I promised to keep an eye on the place, and never give up trying to rescue Mikayla and her boy."

"What about the Harja file?" Cassidy asked. "Ulf may be a crook, but he is knowledgeable about antiques, and was willing to kill and kidnap for more information on the coin Uncle Raglan gave Mikayla. There must be some truth to the treasure's existence."

"Raglan never really filled me in too much on that treasure," Simco said with a shake to his head. "It was like he never really wanted to find it. If he never found it, it was kinda like havin' a goal that he could always search for, and so's if he never found it, he never had to feel his last adventure was over. As a person gets older, sometimes a body feels that way about things. You want to keep a goal just outta reach, so you can keep reaching. It's kinda like saying, "Don't take me yet, Lord, 'cause I'm not ready.""

Cassidy smiled and nodded her head with understanding. She looked at Adam with a fresh sparkle in her eye. "I guess we'll carry his adventure on for him. First, we better pick up Waldo at your uncle's place on Richwood Road, and get that Harja file out of his dog collar. Are you willing to search for some more clues in the rauks, Mr. Lucino?"

"I was hoping you'd ask," Adam grinned a crooked, eager smile.

Cassidy turned to Simco. "It would please me very much if you would care for the mansion while I'm gone."

Simco smiled from ear to ear, and shook his head in agreement. He had grown fond of the Salter River Mansion, and was thrilled to continue his residence there without having to remain hidden. "Can I keep the wolf howl?"

"Well, I suppose it does keep intruders away," Cassidy laughed. "But only when I am not here."

Simco nodded his head in agreement. "Tell Mikayla that old Simco is still alive. I be never forgettin' the horror on her face when Ulf fired his gun, and kicked me off the pier."

***

Lars was not comfortable with the length of time Ulf and Henrik were taking in the Salter River mansion. This was supposed to be a quick deal; drop off the money, pick up the Harja file, and hit back to Sweden as fast as possible. He awaited Ulf's signal to bring the briefcase of money to the house, but when that did not happen as quickly as he anticipated, his suspicious nature took over. A faint glow from the main entrance window rayed into the night, so after a time, Lars decided to peek through the pane to see if everything was going as planned. He brought the stuffed briefcase with him and stepped up onto the veranda platform.

Suddenly, Lars could hear the distant sound of sirens, and darted into a vine covered arbor at the edge of the veranda. He remained still as a statue, concealed by the thick vine branches weaved throughout the latticework. From there, he witnessed the arrest of Ulf and Henrik, and listened to the conversation afterwards by Cassidy, Adam and Simco.

A slight smile passed Lars' lips at the mention of the Harja file being hidden in Adam's dog's collar. He figured that would be easy to retrieve. When Cassidy revealed that Waldo was staying at an address on Richwood Road, Lars felt doubly blessed with information. He would quickly find the location on Richwood Road before any of them arrived there, and retrieve the collar.

Cassidy still had her car parked off to the side of the driveway, where she had left it when she last accompanied Adam in his jeep. The couple took the car to her hotel room where she picked up her belongings and checked out of the room. Then they quickly returned to Adam's residence, collected extra clothes, which both had previously left there, and packed for traveling back to Sweden. Cassidy insisted they stop by the hospital for Adam to have his wounds checked and redressed before retrieving the Harja file from Waldo's collar. Fortunately for Lars, this gave him more spare time than he realized.

Lars did not know of their plans, so felt his time very limited to retrieve the file out of the dog's collar. He had no vehicle, as the police had confiscated their getaway car, so he quickly made his way to a gas station where he signaled a taxi. First, he grabbed a phone book to look up the address of a Lucino living on Richwood Road.

❧ ～ ❧

Ulf had arrived at the Salter River mansion at midnight, so several hours later, it was still dark when Lars stood a short distance from Georgio Lucino's residence on Richwood Road. Adam's uncle owned a large back yard, complete with a long dog kennel run, which temporarily housed Waldo. Lars pondered on how he could approach the dog without the animal barking, and arousing the owner and neighborhood. An idea popped into his head and he walked down the back alley of the street, carrying his briefcase containing twenty million dollars. He walked straight to the first garbage container he could find, opened the lid and fished around for some discarded food that he could bribe a feline with. Sure enough, before long a big friendly cat with an appetite waddled into view.

"Here Miss Kitty…Here Garfie!…Here Oscar!…Here Gingersnap!…Here big stupid orange kitty." The cat finally accepted Lars offer and was soon carried down the street on his hip like a sack of potatoes.

Lars couldn't see over the high wooden fence surrounding the Lucino residence, so found an open knothole to peep through. He was able to distinguish a kennel run on the other side of the barrier, containing a huge dog. He was disappointed at the enormous size of the dog, but figured retrieving the file was worth a dog fight. Having a good tennis swing, Lars flung the surprised cat over the fence into Waldo's domain with ease. Waldo leapt to his feet and began barking at the sudden landing of a cat from the sky. The frightened cat raced back and forth across the yard like a yo-yo, searching for an escape exit, which finally became the open door to the house when Georgio Lucino opened the back door to see what the barking was about. Lights turned on in every corner of the house as the terrified cat ran from room to room, up the stairs and down again with Georgio two feet behind it.

Seeing as Georgio was also looking after Merlin, his brother's cat, while they were in Sweden, a second cat got involved in the chase. Pure bedlam broke loose in the house with Georgio trying to keep one cat in and chase one cat out.

Meanwhile, out in the back yard, Lars quickly tripped the inside lock on the gate, being a criminal skilled in locksmith techniques. He raced to the dog kennel in haste and entered cautiously, speaking softly to the dog. Waldo was thrilled to have someone ruffle his ears and stroke his chin, and Lars was relieved not to get eaten. Lars figured this task was going to be easy until he discovered he could not unbuckle Waldo's collar. Adam had stitched the buckle to the collar to inure Waldo did not lose it, and Lars had no knife to cut the threads.

Hearing the commotion in the house getting closer to ground floor level, and seeing the cat spurt out of the open house door like a cannon ball, Lars decided he could not wait any longer. He slipped the belt out of his pants, used it as a leash to hook around Waldo's collar and lead the dog out of the kennel at a full gallop. He never stopped running with Waldo at his side for an entire six blocks. He then sat down on a park bench and rested the twenty million dollar briefcase beside him. Waldo sat obediently between Lars legs, as the frustrated man turned and twisted the collar as much as he could to try and get it off the dog's lion size head. It was useless to try further. Lars leaned back on the park bench, his two arms limp at his sides in defeat.

"I'd strangle you if I could get my hands around your neck," he cursed, staring into Waldo's big friendly eyes.

Ulf and his men had a flight booked for returning to Sweden, but Lars was unsure whether he should chance taking the flight back or not. If the police knew Ulf, Henrik and himself had traveled as a threesome, they would be waiting at the airport to arrest him. Lars also realized a man with a huge dog would be easily noticed. All he needed was a knife to cut off the dog collar, but that was not easy to find in the middle of the night. He had to get out of sight, but few hotels would accept a dog, and he doubted that any taxi would welcome a dog who took up the whole back seat.

Waldo rose to his feet, gave a loud woof and tried to take off, but Lars belt was still hooked around his collar. "So you want to go home, boy," Lars said to the dog. "Well, lead the way. There'll be a knife there." He slackened his restraint on Waldo's leash and let the dog lead the way home to Adam's house.

It took Lars and Waldo over an hour to walk across the city, over the Salter River Bridge and arrive at Adam's house. Along the way, Lars developed an attachment to the hulk of a hound who innocently trusted Lars' motifs. "It's a good thing you don't have a clue what I am capable of, you big loggerhead," Lars informed Waldo, as the dog affectionately rubbed his jumbo head against Lars' pant leg. Finally, Waldo stopped before Adam's driveway and attempted to approach the house. Lars pulled the dog back into the shadow of trees, and waited across the street until the Lucino house showed no sign of occupation.

～～～

Earlier, Cassidy and Adam had returned to Adam's house, packed clothing for returning to Sweden, and visited the hospital to take care of Adam's wounds. They were now on their way to Richwood Road to obtain Waldo's collar when they received a frantic call from Adam's uncle. "Waldo's gone. Some crazy cat got into the back yard, upset the dog and he broke out of his kennel. Can't find him anywhere."

"He's likely gone home," Adam said. "We'll go back there and check. Call Animal Services in case they have picked him up".

Lars was able to quickly break into the back door of Adam's residence. He did not turn on the lights, but proceeded down the hall to the kitchen to obtain a knife to cut off Waldo's collar. Just as he was about to do so, the lights of a car swung into the driveway and he heard two car doors slam. He heard Adam say, "He's not on the doorstep. I'll check by the garage at the back."

Lars grabbed Waldo's collar and dragged him out the back door and out of sight beside the deck before Adam rounded the corner. He clamped both hands over Waldo's jaws to hold the dog's mouth shut, so he could not bark. Adam checked around the garage and called for Waldo. The dog struggled to bark a response, but Lars desperately kept his hands clamped like a vice on the dog's jaws.

Adam then attempted to unlock the back door and discovered it unlocked. He yelled to Cassidy, "The back door is unlocked. I'm sure I locked it when we left."

"Maybe your uncle was here for something and forgot to lock it," Cassidy suggested, and they both entered the building to check. Cassidy made the mistake of leaving the car running with the keys in the ignition while they made a hasty check in the house. This gave Lars the opportunity to jump into the car with Waldo, and quickly back the vehicle out of the driveway and disappear down the street before Adam and Cassidy realized the car was gone.

Lars knew it would only be a seconds before the car was reported stolen, so driving in the city was not a wise idea. He drove only ten blocks, pulled into an empty lot and shut the car off. He needed to deliberate for a few minutes and figure out a plan before advancing further.

Lars turned to Waldo, and pondered his thoughts aloud to the dog. "I've got twenty million dollars in untraceable Canadian currency in this briefcase. That should be enough for any man...or dog, don't you think?" Waldo gave a throaty woof in agreement.

"Maybe there's a treasure somewhere on Gotland Island worth billions and maybe there's not. But in order to find it, I've got to tramp all over Gotland Island with the police on my tail...and if I take your collar, they'll tie me in with Ulf shooting the taxi driver, and I had nothing to do with that...So big buddy, it looks like you know your way home. Let's hope the law will think the cat simply drove you nuts, and consider the car theft as a separate issue, not anything to do with the file in your collar." He opened the car door and Waldo eagerly jumped out.

"You keep your collar, and all the trouble that goes with it, big buddy. Me and twenty million are on the first bus out of here." He patted Waldo's head, and then ordered the dog, "Go home! Off with you!" Waldo looked at him for a few moments and then took off for home at a full gallop. Lars wiped his fingerprints off the steering wheel and door handles. Then he raised his briefcase to his lips and gave the case a quick kiss, walked across the street and caught a transit bus to the bus depot.

# 19

Adam and Cassidy waited anxiously at Adam's residence for the police to arrive. Cassidy kept trying to reassure Adam that Waldo would be okay, but he feared the worst. "They're the kind of people who don't think twice about shooting a person, so they certainly won't think twice about shooting a dog," Adam expressed in despair.

Adam felt guilty that by involving his dog, he had risked Waldo's life. "They'll kill him to get it off," he moaned to Cassidy "I shouldn't have sewn it so they needed a knife to cut it off. They'll just kill him and take it."

Cassidy wrapped her arms around Adam. "They have no reason to kill Waldo," she said in a comforting voice. "Waldo won't fight them, so they'll just take the collar. That's all they want."

"The police have Ulf and Henrik," Adam deliberated. "Whoever took Waldo must be Matts or Lars. I don't trust Matts. I'm sure he's the one who shot me in the back. He'd shoot a dog just for the fun of it."

"The police in Gotland said three of them came to Canada. Henrik and Lars always seem to be paired up, so I'm thinking Matts was left behind," Cassidy calculated. "Mikayla also told me Lars liked kids, and had stopped Ulf several times from hitting Mikkel when his noisy playing annoyed Ulf. That's good news for Waldo. People who like kids usually like dogs."

Just as the police pulled into Adam's driveway, Waldo came flying down the street, tail wagging and tongue flapping like a red flag. He practically knocked Adam over in his joy to see his owner. Adam hugged the dog like one hugging a lost child. Then he grabbed his collar and threw Cassidy a puzzled look. The collar had not been removed. "I guess we were wrong about Lars kidnapping him for the collar. Waldo must have broken out of Uncle's kennel when the cat got in the back yard. Guess your car being stolen had nothing to do with Waldo's collar. That's a relief."

A very apologetic Uncle Georgio rushed to once again pick up Waldo. "I still can't figure out how he got out of that kennel, and how the back gate got unlocked. Doesn't make sense. From now on, Waldo doesn't leave my side until you get back from Sweden. We'll eat and sleep together, share steak, and he can even sit beside me at my workshop."

Waldo was quite okay with the steak-sharing part.

As they spoke to the police about the stolen car, a call came in to the officer. He informed Cassidy that her car had already been located only ten blocks away, undamaged with the keys still in it. Georgio agreed to pick up the car after the police released it, so once again, Cassidy sighed with relief.

Adam glanced at his wrist watch. "We had better hurry if we are to catch our flights back to Sweden. I'll remove the Harja file from Waldo's collar and then we better hit the airport." All four crowded into Uncle Georgio's vehicle, including Waldo who stretched across Cassidy's lap.

Dawn was beginning to lighten the sky as Cassidy rested her head upon Waldo's. It had been quite a night with the arrest of Ulf and Henrik, the discovery of Simco, the disappearance and return of Waldo and the theft and finding of her car. She had not even had time to call her mother, and she did so now.

Cassidy informed her mother that she was safe, the criminals caught, and that she was returning to Sweden to see if Uncle Raglan's tales of a pirate treasure were true. It was one of those rare moments when all seemed well with the world.

Cassidy and Adam leaned their heads back on the airplane seats almost simultaneously. They turned their weary faces toward each other. "Do you realize we haven't slept since arriving in Canada?" Cassidy moaned.

"Yes!" Adam agreed. "We packed a lot of drama into one day, didn't we? Finding Simco alive and that he was the ghost of the Salter River Mansion was awesome. Guess we better sleep because there won't be a moment's rest when we meet my parents and Mikayla at the ferry landing. You know, I can't thank your doctor friend enough for what he's done to help my family."

"My father saved his father's life in the war, so I think Dr. Neilsson is thoroughly enjoying repaying the favor."

150

"From what my Mama told me on the phone, it sounds like him and Mikayla are hitting it off pretty good."

Cassidy's face beamed. "Oh, wouldn't it be nice if they became a couple. Dad says he's a very good person, and I could see he was attracted to Mikayla right from the beginning. It would also be good for Mikkel to have a loving father. I don't think Ulf showed Mikkel any affection at all. Your sister and her son also love the island. I can tell by the way she talks about the historic fossils and such. They sort of belong on Gotland Island, don't you think?" Cassidy paused for a second and then laughed, "…Just call me a romantic."

"With some people," Adam mumbled partly under his breath, and closed his eyes as if in slumber.

It was raining heavily when the couple exited the plane, picked up their suitcases, and hit for the line-up of people waiting for taxis and shuttle buses. As they had several hours to wait for a connection to the ferry crossing times, Adam stepped out of the line and moved to the side. "We might as well let these people go first. We have a couple hours to wait before needing connections to the ferry."

Cassidy nodded in agreement, and moved to the side of the advancing crowd, all anxiously seeking transportation out of the rain to their destinations.

Adam stood near the platform roof where the rain was

pouring over the eaves like Niagara Falls. He silently watched people popping up umbrellas and running in haste to climb into vehicles. Suddenly, he spoke very precisely. "So, I suppose we're not considered engaged anymore...seeing as you returned my ring."

Cassidy's eyes jolted open in surprise, and her mouth dropped open. "I...uh...returned your sister's ring...not your engagement ring."

His eyes slanted as he peered at her from beneath the rim of his hat. "I suppose...if that's the way you want to look at it." Thunder boomed and rain fell even heavier, single raindrops no longer bouncing off taxi roof tops, but pouring over the vehicles like melted butter.

He remembered how his heart completely stopped when she kissed him in the farm house after he had given her the bracelet. If she had no interest in him, he wished he knew, for then he would make sure he didn't sit so close as to be jealous of the little strand of hair that always seemed to curl down and brush her lips.

She viewed him peering out into the rain with a discouraged look about his shoulders. She could tell there was a battle going on inside of him, and there was a battle going on inside of her, as well. One part was saying, "If you want us engaged, then why don't you ask me to marry you", and the other part was saying, "Don't you dare ask me to marry you because I hardly know you...other than being the greatest guy I ever met."

She couldn't explain why she did it, unless it was to disintegrate the confusion in her head, but Cassidy gave Adam a hefty shove out onto the platform into the pouring rain. The wind whipped his hat off into the street, and it landed amongst the traffic. A taxi hurrying by, ground Adam's hat into the runoff water and mud like a squashed melon.

"What the hell!" Adam cried, rain pouring down his face and flattening his otherwise spiked hair. "Are you crazy?" The rain traveled down his long, tan trench coat, and sufficed as an umbrella over his shoes, which were the only articles left dry on Adam's body.

People waiting for taxis under the shelter of the airport overhang, began to notice the young couple who appeared to be having an argument. Some snickered at the young man, drenched to the bone, standing on the platform in obvious shock at his girlfriend pushing him out into the torrential rain.

Cassidy reached out and grabbed a fistful of his jacket at the throat and yanked him back in out of the rain. She pulled his head down and kissed his lips, tasting the rain, moist and seductive upon them. Adam could think of nothing to say when she let him go. "You're wet," she whispered, as droplets dripped off the ends of his spiked hair and fell upon the freckles on her nose.

Adam shook his finger at her. "And you're wicked!"

<hr />

The couple waited at the ferry crossing for departure time. The rain had stopped and now they sipped coffee while seated at a small outdoor table. They had said very little to each other since leaving the airport. Cassidy was thinking that she shouldn't have kissed Adam like that, and Adam was thinking that he had no idea why she had.

Adam spread his trench coat out to dry across two chairs in the sunshine. "You owe me a hat," he finally blurted.

Cassidy smiled, and studied him from across the table. "Sorry! I thought you were acting a bit…twitter patted…but then you looked like such a pitiful, wet dog, I decided to rescue you."

"It's not considered a rescue if you throw someone under the train first," Adam said in a harsh, scolding tone.

She laughed mischievously and sat her coffee cup down. "Speaking of dogs, I have decided I know more about Waldo than I do about you. What do you do when your day of grounds keeping is over?"

Adam inhaled deeply. "Well, let's see. Although grounds keeping is my favorite part of the job, I am also manager and co-owner of the apartment complex in partnership with my father and uncle. On days off, I golf a little, fish a little, and spend a lot of time at my recreational center. It's a place that I own and run for kids to keep them off the streets after school."

Adam was eager to speak about a cause so close to his heart. "I bought this old warehouse about four years ago, and turned it into a place for kids to go to after school. Volunteers like my parents and uncle, a few friends, parents, and myself take turns supervising from 4 to 8 o'clock every evening, including weekends. I installed basketball hoops, goalie nets and bought other recreational equipment. Most of the parents in that area don't have the money to put their kids in organized sports, but they can help supervise, even if just for an hour here or there, and it gives them a sense of participation. Makes for a better bond with their kids. Some of the kids come from broken homes, even abusive situations, but it gives them a happy, more constructive place to escape to for a while."

Cassidy nodded her head in approval from across the table. "That's amazing. I'm so proud of you. Those kids must adore you."

"Well, I don't know about that," Adam laughed. "They beat this bum leg up pretty bad, playing floor hockey…I think Uncle Georgio is their favorite. He's a cabinet builder, so comes down with spare wood and holds wood classes. He teaches the kids how to use different tools by having them build bird houses and dog houses, even cabinets and tables. The kids sell them after and make some extra money for themselves. He says he's training future competitors."

Cassidy listened with keen interest and admiration for such a worthy cause.

"We have one native grandmother who offers native art classes on Tuesdays," he continued, "and a bike shop owner who demonstrates bike repair and safety once a month. The police even bring down a police dog occasionally to build a good relationship between the law and the kids…It's a good place…I'm going to buy the lot next door and build an outdoor hockey rink someday too…when I have enough saved. Well, enough about me. Tell me what you do after you've pulled teeth all day."

"Let's see! I took dance lessons until Mom had her accident," Cassidy revealed somewhat shyly. "Then I stayed home a lot with my mother, so switched to taking piano lessons. Mom is an excellent piano player, so I had a built-in teacher. Trouble was, Mom said music was in my toes, not my fingers...Oh, but I am interested in older architecture, and would love to restore the Salter River Mansion. I like river rafting...and camping...I cook a mean marshmallow over the campfire."

Adam laughed. "Miss Leslie, I do think you have many hidden talents that I am going to enjoy discovering...Maybe someday you might find time to offer a few dance lessons to my kids at the center."

Suddenly, the ferry arrived, and they hurried to board.

# 20

The welcoming party of the Lucino family and Daniel gathered at the ferry docks on Gotland Island. Little Mikkel, feeding off the excitement of his grandparents and mother, waved two balloons vigorously at Cassidy and Adam, as they stepped off the ferry. Hugs were in order for everyone, and the celebration was even greater because they felt Ulf was behind bars, and no longer a threat to them.

"I couldn't bring Big Bear because Mommy said there was no room in the car, so I left him home," Mikkel explained earnestly to Adam. Adam remembered Cassidy telling him about the big stuffed Polar Bear that his parents had given Mikkel. The reference to Dr. Neilsson's house as "home" did not go unnoticed, and Adam hoped the boy would not get hurt by embracing a place that might not be permanent. He shook off the concern. Today, there was only room for the celebration and reunion of family.

After lunch, the family relaxed outside on the garden patio, entertained by Mikkel giving wagon rides to Nicolass, the cat. Adam, however, was unusually quiet. Mikayla could see worried frown lines on her brother's forehead, as he observed the boy playing so contently in the yard, so she brought the issue of her marriage status into the conversation.

"I've spoken to the authorities here," Mikayla informed

Adam. "Dad and Daniel helped me obtain a lawyer, and I have filed for divorce. I do not think I will have any problem getting full custody of Mikkel, once Ulf is legally sentenced as a dangerous criminal. I had thought of trying to obtain an annulment, seeing as I was kidnapped and forced into marriage, but that might affect Mikkel. I have to get a passport for him, and Ulf is still legally his father."

Mikayla sighed. "I would like to have this nightmare over with once and for all, but there are legal channels that have to be followed. As Ulf's wife, I might be entitled to a percentage of his assets after our divorce, if he has anything legal left, but I want nothing. If he was ever released from prison, he would come looking for every penny that I took. I also realize that Matts and Lars were not arrested with Ulf and Henrik, so they are out there somewhere, perhaps still doing business for him. I predict Henrik will not be charged with an attempt on Simco's life, as he was not in Canada at that time. He may get out of jail sooner than we think."

Mikayla walked to where Adam was sitting, and ruffled his hair affectionately, a sisterly gesture she had not done for years. "I want nothing that might give Ulf or his men reason to search for Mikkel or myself. I know he owes me big for five years of hell and fear of what he might do to Mikkel, but I don't want to spend the rest of my life scared of shadows because I took anything from him."

Mikayla's voice trembled for a moment, her calm composure suddenly broken. Within seconds, she took a deep breath and straightened her shoulders again, not wanting Mikkel to notice her upset. "Dad and Mama, and the police came with me to cancel our lease on the penthouse, so the building owners will not be expecting further payments from Ulf. I took only my passport from his vault, a few clothes and personal belongings such as my pirate coin necklace that Raglan Leslie gave me, and a few toys that Mikkel was attached to. The rest is Ulf's...and the laws. It is no further concern of mine." She touched her throat where the simple string with an old pirate's coin hung. "I didn't even take one diamond ear-ring."

Mikayla walked to the edge of the patio to call Mikkel back with the cat in the wagon. "Erica, my bodyguard has completely disappeared, along with a diamond necklace and ear-ring set worth twenty thousand that Ulf told everyone was my wedding gift. Ulf will blame me for taking them, but I'm glad if Erica took it. It's probably the first sparkle she ever owned in her life. She was trying to escape Ulf's clutches ever since she met some man that Ulf didn't like. In a way, she helped me escape, so I owe her the necklace."

Mikayla lifted Nicolass out of the wagon. "I think kitty is getting thirsty, sweetheart," she smiled at Mikkel. "We'll give him a rest for a while. Okay! You go get him a glass of milk and pour it in his dish."

Mikkel nodded, and ran off happily to oblige his mother's wishes.

"Seems like you've been doing a lot of thinking since I've been gone," Adam said. "You do whatever you feel is right for you and the boy. If you need money, we are here for you. If you need a place, we have a large apartment complex to choose from, free of charge until you get your life back together. You don't need to worry about where to live."

Mikayla smiled and threw a quick shy glance at Daniel Neilsson. "Well…your offer is greatly appreciated, Adam, and trust me, when we visit, we will grab one of those empty apartments…but I have business here…until we get legal matters settled. Dr. Neilsson…Daniel…has graciously offered his country home to Mikkel and I until we can get things in order. Mikkel has been having nightmares of his father chasing and catching him in the goat shed. He seems to feel safe if we let Daniel's cat sleep on his bed, so maybe it is best not to uproot Mikkel right now."

Dr. Neilsson had been quiet, listening to the conversations, not wanting to interfere with the bonding of family, or any decisions they may be making, but now he thought was a good time to intervene. "You are all welcome to stay as long as you wish and need. There's a couple rooms above the garage, which we can fix up for more guests, so there's a spot to sleep for everyone…Now, Mr. and Mrs. Lucino and I are hitting the open market this afternoon if anyone wants to join us and chose foods for tonight's menu. We'll exchange Italian and Swedish recipes tonight."

All agreed to go except Cassidy and Adam who were tired from their flight, and looked forward to a few hours of quiet relaxation.

Adam wandered across the lawn, down to a pond where a couple white ducks circled in the middle, trying to catch a busy water beetle. The day was humid, so he removed his shirt and shoes, and walked along the shore of the pond in knee-length shorts, cooling his feet in the water. He had a lot to think about; Mikayla's situation, the treasure they would start searching for again tomorrow, and most of all, he had Cassidy to think about.

Cassidy watched him from the patio for a time, enjoying the restful scene of Adam wading along the shore in silhouette with glistening waters behind him. She finally decided to join him. She walked slowly down the incline to the pond, removed her shoes, and walked along the shore toward Adam, her skirt tucked up into her waistband, so as not to get wet. When they met face to face, a smile of greeting passed between them. "Are you prepared to hunt for treasure tomorrow?" Cassidy asked cheerfully. "It will be so nice to search for clues without bullets aimed at us…Speaking of bullets, how is your side?"

Adam was shirtless and she noted the bandage taped over his injury. She reached out and rested her palm gently upon his wound. He flinched, but it was not from the wound. "You should get Daniel to look at that tonight," Cassidy advised with concern in her eyes.

Adam said nothing, so Cassidy carried on the conversation herself. She turned to walk beside him along the shore. She thought his unusual quietness was due to worry over his sister. "Don't worry about Mikayla staying here," she assured him. "She's a smart lady who knows what she wants. She has had to do what was best for Mikkel for four years…and I don't think Daniel will take advantage of her situation."

"Not a good idea to trust a man who is twitter-patted," Adam warned, and swooped her up and dropped her like a sack of potatoes into the cool pond water.

Cassidy scrambled to her feet, spitting water and gasping for air, mad as a wet hen. She shook both fists at him while tossing her head to whip wet bangs out of her eyes. She was completely soaked from head to toe, and blubbered death threats, even though she realized he had done this in retaliation for the airport soaking.

"Payback time," Adam grinned, and swept her into his strong, muscled arms, holding her to his chest in a tight vice. Then he lowered his lips and kissed her. The kiss was meant to be in innocent fun, but instead, it stirred deep emotions in both of them. Suddenly, both realized they had stepped beyond friendship, and he quickly released his arms about her.

Cassidy hurried toward her room to change her wet clothing, and then turned around to face Adam once again. "Maybe we could print out the treasure map from the Harja file, now that Ulf is not a danger to us." She was looking for any topic to clear the awkwardness in the air between them.

He nodded in agreement. "Good idea!"

Both tried to act like nothing had changed in their friendship. She wanted to say something about their embrace but what can you say about feeling something so wonderfully intoxicating that you shouldn't be feeling. They stared at each other for a couple minutes, neither speaking, just absorbing the memory of passion that had passed between them. You don't forget moments of desire. You can explain it away with a million excuses, but you don't forget it. She inhaled slowly and turned toward her room.

Adam removed a bottle of red wine from Daniel's wine

cooler, and poured himself a glass of wine. He took a sip and closed his eyes, savoring the taste of plum and tangy pepper. He could still feel Cassidy against his chest and wondered if the feeling would ever go away…and not wanting it to.

Matts clutched the phone, relieved to finally hear Henrik's voice from Canada. Matts had learned earlier that Ulf was arrested for attempted murder, but knew little else.

"I'm out on bail for the moment" Henrik explained. "I wasn't in the country five years ago when Ulf shot Simco and kidnapped Mikayla, so there's no attempted murder charge on me. Ulf bought weapons from some crooked dealer over here, and I had a weapon on me at the mansion, so might get charged for possession and abetting Ulf, but I never uttered threats to Simco. Ulf did all the talking. Have to appear in court next week. Has Lars been in contact with you? He's got the twenty million."

"What do you mean Lars has the twenty million?" Matts echoed back in shock, for he had not received a single word from Lars.

"He must have took off with the money when he saw the police coming", Henrik surmised. "We haven't heard or seen a hair of him since. Do you think the sucker would take off with Ulf's twenty million?"

Matts deliberated only for a second. "Let's face it, Henrik. Not too much honor between thieves. The money was all in untraceable Canadian currency. Ulf made sure of that. Twenty million could get Lars out of the country and let him live a pretty good life."

"Ulf will kill him," Henrik spat out. "He'll track him down like a dog."

"Not my problem," Matts expressed nonchalantly on the phone. "I'm not about to wait around for Ulf to get out of prison, if he ever does. I plan to get me that pirate's treasure while the boss is counting bars on the window, and then I won't need him anymore."

"What about me?" Henrik's voice squeaked in dismay, realizing he was now out of a job with Ulf arrested, and there was a great possibility he may be behind bars himself for a while.

"Not my problem either," Matts repeated with cool indifference. "Your bad luck, not mine. I can't wait for you. The kids are back over here looking for the treasure already. If you get over here in time, I'll cut you in. Otherwise, as soon as they locate the treasure, or I get my hands on the map, I'll see to it that they disappear in the Baltic, while I hit for some place far away with my loot. Good luck to you." Matts hung up the phone.

# 21

Cassidy and Adam studied the Harja file in closer detail, as they had little chance to study the map previously. They printed the map out from the computer, so they could take it along on their journey in search of the treasure. When first discovering the file, they had wasted no time hiding the memory card in Waldo's collar, and only memorized a quick overview of the map. Now, having discovered that fossils in the rauks resembled the daggers on the map, it made the map much more understandable.

"Before Matts waved that gun in our faces, I discovered three fossils on a rauk, one above the other like the three daggers on this diagram," Cassidy remembered with excitement, pointing to the position on the map. "So that must be the starting point."

"Continuing on from the fossils, it shows an arrow pointing to an area near a spot marked LC. I wonder what LC stands for."

Mikayla was busy tossing a salad for supper with her mother, and spoke up, "Lummelunda Caves." They all turned and stared at her. "Just a wild guess," she said, waving a stir spoon around in her hand with Italian flair. "That area has many gullies, caves and sink holes formed by the tide rising and falling and carving the sedimentary rocks over thousands of years. It can be a dangerous place to explore if you aren't careful."

"A perfect place for hiding treasure," Cassidy exploded with fresh adrenalin.

"Not exactly," Mikayla dampened her spirits. "The tide waters would destroy and wash away treasure on the shore lines, but Captain Skully might have found a protected spot above the tide level for his treasure. Old tales say he had no less than a dozen such treasures buried on the island, but only the one was guarded by his runic dagger."

Adam studied the map further. "The map also shows a curvy S in front of three triangles by the coast line. Guess we'll have to scout out the area and see what we can find that resembles those symbols."

The following morning, Cassidy and Adam filled their backpacks with tools for an expedition and mounted their motorcycle. They decided to first recheck their fossil find in the rauks and determine what significance the dagger-like fossils held to the area around the Lummelunda Caves.

After examining the rauks and being reassured that the fossils resembling daggers were identical to the clues on the map, they hit for an area around the Lummelunda Caves. They parked the bike high on a hillside, knowing that the tide would eventually be coming in, and they did not want their transportation swept away. They climbed down the rocky slopes, continuing to search for anything resembling an S formation. Finally, they rested on a large rock to eat lunch.

Adam took a bite from a sandwich and apologized, "I'm sorry about yesterday. I was just paying you back for pushing me into the rain at the airport. As you said before, we're not really...compatible."

Cassidy nodded. "Well, the next time we get kidding around, I think we better leave kissing out of it." She could not look at him as she spoke, because in truth, she was savoring the memory.

Adam sighed somewhat sadly, and reached into his bag for another sandwich. "Yeah! You're right...because we're kinda getting good at it."

Cassidy's cheeks flushed and she hurried to eat the rest of her lunch. She had found it difficult all day not to steal glances at him. She wasn't sure why she was fighting her magnetism towards him. He was a great guy. Maybe it was the mystery of never knowing what he was capable of that kept her at a distance...or maybe it was memories of an old boyfriend who once told her she didn't measure up to his expectations, and she feared Adam might someday come to the same conclusion.

The sedimentary rocks where they sat to eat lunch had been worn smooth from the tide, and Adam used one as a table to spread the treasure map upon. Unknown to the young couple, Matts watched their every move with powerful binoculars. Seeing Adam display the map on the rock sparked Matts' hope in finding the treasure for himself. He quickly pulled a mask over his face to appear as an elderly man with gray hair and beard, and drove closer to where Adam and Cassidy examined the map. He climbed down from the rocks above until he was a short distance from them. Then he hollered, "Hello there, young folk. I'm afraid I'm lost. Went for a hike and got turned about somehow. Would you be able to explain how to get back to Hillstep Road?"

Adam quickly folded the map and stuffed it in his back pocket, and reached out a hand to help the elderly looking gentleman down onto their cliff shelf. Once abreast, Adam could see the man was wearing a disguise, but it was too late for him to react. Matts whipped off his mask in a flash, withdrew a gun and pointed it at Adam's chest. He ordered Adam to hand over the map, and Adam had no choice but to obey.

Matts smiled with devilish pleasure. "Folks will think you both forgot about the tide and were swept out to sea. No one will know we even met."

Realizing that Matts had no intension of leaving them alive, Adam attempted a small chance at survival. As he reached out to hand Matts the folded map, he quickly swiped at the gun with the map, and knocked it out of Matts' hand. The two men wrestled on the rocks, rolling to and fro, each trying to get a lasting hold on the other. Cassidy looked about for anything to hit Matts with, but the sea had washed even the smallest pebble away. The gun had slipped over the cliff shelf, and she could not reach it. All she had for a weapon was her hands and shoes.

The larger and stronger Matts pinned Adam to the ground at the edge of the cliff shelf, and wrapped his strangling fingers around Adam's throat. Cassidy jumped on Matts' back, yanking at his hair, hitting him on the back of the head with her shoe, and pounding him with all the strength her small fists could muster. She was no match for Matts' strength. He half turned and smashed her on the side of the face. Cassidy fell back, stunned on the ground from his blow. Her brave act, however, had allowed Adam time to grab Matt's shirt by the chest and heave him over the cliff.

All was quiet for a few minutes as Cassidy and Adam sat in relief and gasped for breath. Adam attempted to look over the cliff, expecting to see Matts unconscious or dead on the shelf below, but cautious Cassidy grabbed him by the arm and shook her head. She grabbed her shoe and whispered to Adam to hold it out over the cliff. He did so gingerly.

"Ping," went a bullet and her shoe flew in the air like a clay pigeon, with a bullet hole through the toe. "You're both dead when I get up there," Matts yelled. "You have no place to go."

The couple looked around. All that lied above was smooth rock with no climbing foot holes. To the left, one large boulder sat more upright in contrast to other flatter rocks, and created the only hope out of the area, other than climbing down into Matts' domain. "I think I can hoist myself up on that big protruding rock to the left," Adam said in desperation. "Then I'll pass down my belt and pull you up. We'll try to jump over to that small shelf along the left side of the smooth boulder. We've got to hurry. He'll be up here in a few minutes."

Adam managed to hoist himself up onto the upright boulder. He balanced on top for a second, then his feet slipped out from beneath him and he disappeared behind the protruding rock. Cassidy ran to where he had fallen, hearing him moan in pain mysteriously from somewhere far below. Behind the large rock was a sinkhole entrance about the size of a car tire. Adam had slipped and fallen down the tunnel shaft into a cave hollowed out by tide waters over the centuries. She could see him lying on his side, rocking back and forth, grasping his injured leg in pain. She feared he had broken it.

Cassidy slid her way down the shaft to where Adam was laying. She did not consider the fact that there were no foot holes or way to climb back out. The tunnel sides had been buffed to a high glaze by the tide waters. All she could think of was to reach Adam and see how badly he was hurt.

Suddenly, Matts' laughter roared from above. "Aaaah, so I've caught two gophers, or should I say goldfish. What luck! I won't even have to waste a bullet. The tide will be coming in pretty soon and will fill that cave like a fish bowl." He laughed viciously again. "Man, I couldn't have planned this better if I tried. Now, I'm just going to watch for a while, to make sure no little gopher peeks his head out of the hole until the tide rolls in…Thanks for the map."

Adam sat upright slowly, and looked at her with a blood stained, defeated face, which he had acquired from slamming his head onto the cave's rock floor. She reached out her hand to help him to his feet. He held his side as he struggled to stand on one leg, trying not to put pressure on his injured one. She could see bruised marks on his neck where Matts had tried to strangle him, the cut on his forehead beginning to swell from his awkward fall into the cave basin, and now drops of blood staining his shirt where he had been shot weeks before.

Tears filled Cassidy's eyes. "Look what I've done to you. You're a bloody disaster…I don't want that stupid treasure anymore."

Adam tried to smile through his pain. "No time for tears. We've got to do some fast thinking. The way I see it, there's got to be a drain hole somewhere in this fish bowl. Otherwise, it would be full of water. It's fairly dark in here, but feel around the edges and see if you can find an outlet for the water. Maybe it will be big enough for us to escape out of."

It didn't take long in the small space for them to discover a small tunnel merely the size of a stove pipe, where the water eventually drained back out to sea. "Okay, that escape route is out," Adam declared in disappointment. "There are no foot holes to climb up out of here that I can see. The sides feel smooth as glass, and too far apart to straddle and work your way up the tunnel. When the tide starts pouring in, it will rush down like a waterfall, so would wash us back down if we tried to climb out while it was pouring in, and Matts will shoot us if we try to get out before the tide comes in."

"Do you think we could stay afloat long enough to wait until the cave is almost full, and let the water carry us up to the opening? "Cassidy asked. "Then we could swim out through the hole. We'd have to stay afloat until the cave is full. That might take a while."

"I'm no English Channel swimmer, but it might be our only chance. We can help each other, and hold onto the walls for some support. I think we can do it. Let's just hope he's not out there to pop a shot at us when we swim out."

"I think once the tide is pouring in here, he'll have to beat it himself, or get swept away."

Cassidy sat down on the ground and beckoned Adam to do likewise. "We better rest our legs, as we might be swimming for a long time. How badly is your leg hurt?"

"I don't think it's broken." Adam massaged his sore knee. "You know, I am beginning to understand how your uncle felt about keeping a few adventures in reserve. One should really spread your adventures out, don't you think? I think we've filled our quota this month."

Cassidy laughed, despite realizing they were in a possible death situation. She reached out to touch his shoulder, being comforted simply to feel his body near her in the shadows. Only a sunbeam from the sinkhole entrance, and a small hole in the ceiling of the dome roof shone down to offer slight light in the cave bowl. They could hear the roar of tidal waves hitting the rocks below, its rumble approaching like an oncoming train.

Adam could sense Cassidy's fears mount, so thought of something to take her mind off the approaching tide. "What broke you up with your old boyfriend?"

Cassidy's eyes saddened at the memory of words once received. "He said I was too... predictable. He wanted someone more...exciting and rebellious...more dangerous. Me! A dentist! He had the nerve to call a dentist not dangerous? I should have pulled all his teeth out."

Adam laughed out loud, recalling a feisty Cassidy pounding Matts' back with her shoe like a wildcat. He could not imagine anyone thinking she was predictable. "You are the most fascinating and exciting lady I have ever met, Miss Leslie. You surprise me every day. He lost a real prize."

"Thank you, Mr. Lucino! That made my day...such as it

is," Cassidy said graciously, looking about at their possible tomb if they were not able to swim out successfully. "What happened to all your ladies?"

Adam changed positions with his leg and moaned slightly as pain knifed through his knee. "I had a few girls when I was a college hockey star...before the gimpy leg and broken nose...Funny how something like that can completely define you as a different person overnight."

An evil laugh suddenly echoed down the sink hole. "Tide is in." Then Matts sang a little mocking tune as he left the couple to their fate. Gradually his voice faded into the roar of the tide.

# 22

They waited and knew the tide would soon reach the cave opening high above them. Waiting was a combination of not wanting the ordeal to begin, and wanting it to begin so they could deal with it. Cassidy pressed her hands together and held them to her lips in silent prayer.

The water poured down the opening in a sudden rush of a waterfall, and then stopped as the waves receded before the next tidal wave drove to shore. They remained seated as long as they could, and watched the water pour in with shorter intervals between the waves, raising the water level about them until they had to stand on their feet, and prepare for swimming.

Adam yelled to her. "Get over as close as you can to the wall beneath the opening, and use the wall for support. I'll be beside you. If you get tired, float on your back and I'll help you rest. Then I'll take a turn."

It wasn't long before the water poured in non-stop, gradually filling the cave bowl. The cave became dark except for the small opening in the ceiling, which created a frightening cocoon atmosphere. Only a faint glow at the sinkhole entrance guided them to a spot for escape.

Cassidy reached out constantly to touch Adam to make

sure he was near. "I'm afraid we might run out of air to breathe, Adam. With the water pouring in, not a drop of oxygen is getting in here. We'll suffocate before we can swim out."

"I think that little opening at the top of this cave will give us enough oxygen until the tide covers our entrance hole. Then we have to get out fast. Now listen carefully. Try to float up behind the waterfall coming in, so you will be close to the entrance when this cave basin is full. I don't think we'll have enough strength left to swim out against the force of the water pouring in, so we'll wait. As soon as the flow stops pouring in, I'll give you a shove up toward the tunnel entrance. You swim as hard and fast as you can to get out. Don't hesitate because I won't have any air left."

Cassidy was terrified that Adam might not make it, as he had to hold his breath under water until she swam out of the tunnel entrance, and then follow her. She could not bear the thought of losing him. In a shaky voice, she cried out, "I love you, Adam."

"Then swim with all the strength you've got left. When you're out, put your back quickly to that upright rock. Then you won't be swept back out to sea. Wait for me and watch your footing, so you don't kick me back down into this hole. Otherwise, I won't be able to hold my breath until I find the tunnel opening again."

Adam and Cassidy pressed their backs as far as they could behind the fall of water, their bodies rising upward with the water level. Soon the top of their heads touched the cave ceiling. When the water level almost reached their nostrils, they both sucked in a final deep breath of air, and Adam shoved Cassidy up the tunnel entrance. She knew she had to swim fast to give Adam chance to also swim out of the hole, as he could not hold his breath for long.

She discovered the water only up to her waist when she escaped the sinkhole entrance, and pressed her back to the upright boulder, as he had instructed. Within seconds, Adam also emerged from the hole, gasping for air as he swam to the surface. He had swallowed water and now stood beside her, coughing and looking pale.

Adam scanned around quickly and counted the seconds between waves hitting the back side of the boulder. He looked in the distance, and studied the rocks they had once slid so easily down after leaving their motorcycle at the top. His head felt dizzy and he could barely bend his one knee, but he kept silent about his injured condition. If Cassidy concentrated on him, she might not concentrate enough on reaching the farther destination.

He pointed a finger at a ledge running along the left side of the smooth rocks. "Once we get onto that ledge, we can climb safely above the tide. I've counted about fifteen seconds between the waves. Get ready, and I'll give you a signal when the next wave is hitting. Then you swim as fast as you can, and let the current help carry you to that ledge. You've got to climb up on the ledge quickly before the current drags you back."

Cassidy was not enthusiastic about his idea. "Oh Adam, I feel like jelly after trying to stay afloat for so long in the cave. Can we not just wait here until the tide goes down? The water is only up to our waists."

"Do you see that band of crusty moss on those smooth rocks high above our heads to the right?"

Cassidy nodded her head.

"Well that's the tide level."

Cassidy prepared herself for his signal, and the second the incoming tide brought a strong wave, Cassidy used the force to send her body soaring like a surfer toward the cliff face and ledge. Adam waited in agony as he watched her struggle for the last six feet, fighting against the waves receding back toward the sea. She reached the rock face and pulled herself up on the ledge in victory.

Thinking Adam stronger than herself, Cassidy had little concern that he might not be as successful as she. She had no idea that he would have to struggle immensely to make the final swim to safety. It was only when Adam rested his forehead in the palm of his hand, that she realized something was wrong. A surge of fear grasped her chest, for she knew he had smashed his head on the cave basin floor when he fell into the sink hole, and had also injured his leg. If he did not swim fast enough to reach the ledge before the tide receded, he would be lost. The thunderous waves made it impossible to carry on a conversation. She wanted to yell encouragement to him but could only wait. She noted the tide had now risen to his chest, and whispered into the roar of the sea, "Come on, Adam. Come on…Come on."

Adam tried to bend his injured leg, only to discover his knee painfully stiff. He would need strong arms and the force of a high wave to carry him to Cassidy. He waited until he could see an oncoming powerful wave, and dove forward with it, using his arms to propel himself through the water to the cliff face. Cassidy reached down as far as she dared without falling off the cliff shelf, and grabbed his wrist to draw him up the last step to safety.

Fearful that Matts may still be about, they proceeded to climb as quickly as they could to where their motorcycle waited. Adam could put little weight on his injured leg, so he practically dragged himself up the climb. Once reaching the crest, he collapsed to the ground, and lay motionless.

"We can't stay here," Cassidy cried, shaking his collapsed body. "Matts might be out here checking with his stolen map. There's also a storm coming."

Adam had spent his last ounce of energy escaping with injuries, and was now limp from exhaustion and pain. He closed eyes and mumbled softly. "Just a few minutes. Let me rest…just a few minutes." His breathing came deeper and deeper and she realized he had fallen asleep.

⁓

Cassidy resigned to giving him five minutes rest. Her head darted in every direction, watching like a hawk for the slightest sound of anyone approaching. She walked over to the drop off and stared down at the swirling waters of the incoming tide. The water caused fluffy foam to wrap in and about the rocks like a long white scarf. Cassidy noted that the foam created an S formation along the shoreline in front of three cliff peaks. Did the foam of the sea represent the S on the treasure map?

Adam moaned and sat upright. He looked about and dragged himself to his feet, keeping his weight off his injured leg.

She stood the bike upright, and bid him mount on behind her, as he looked about to fall over again. Adam's eyes squinted doubtfully but she assured him, "I've got quite good on this thing."

A flash of lightning whipped across the sky and thunder followed almost simultaneously. Cassidy looked skyward. "I don't want to be riding in lightning. I'm hitting for the old house."

They pushed the bike into the old country cottage and shut the door quickly against the wind and sudden fall of heavy rain. Cassidy pushed a chair under Adam, so he could get off his leg and threw some wood in the stove. With a smug little face she opened a cupboard and drew out matches, a blanket concealed in a plastic bag, a tin of Irish stew and a can opener.

Adam stared in surprise as Cassidy explained. "I thought we might need our little hideaway again someday, so I hid a few items." She lit the fire in the stove, opened the can of stew and sat the tin on the stove to heat up. Then she opened the plastic bag and wrapped the blanket around Adam."

Adam removed three pieces of a smashed cell phone from his pocket. "It would be nice to let my folks know we are all right, but I'm afraid the phone is finished."

"As soon as this storm is over, we'll hit for Dr. Neilsson's, or they'll be sending the whole army out looking for us," Cassidy said, stirring the stew in the can on the stove. "I doubt if Matts will be on the road before dawn. Matts believes we're drowned, so he's going to be feeling pretty confident, which makes him a whole lot easier for the law to catch."

After eating, the couple spread the blanket on the hard wooden floor, and settled down to rest until the storm was over. Adam invited her to snuggle up against him for warmth. After a quiet time, Adam casually mentioned, "When I was five, my sister made me eat dirt because I threw a pebble at a bird."

Cassidy snickered, and looked up into his face, so close to hers. "Well, sounds like you deserved it."

Adam smiled at her lack of sympathy. "Yes, and I never forgot the lesson. So good night, Cassy!"

# 23

Dr. Neilsson and the Lucino family poured out of the house with cries of relief at the sound of Cassidy and Adam's motorcycle puttering up to the front door step. Their arms waved vigorously like fans celebrating a winning home game. The men instantly assisted Adam into the house with his injured leg, and waited anxiously for a full explanation of what had happened.

Dr. Neilsson wasted no time in requesting Adam have a shower, put on some clean clothes, and prepare for going to the hospital to get an x-ray on his leg, and have his head injury and former gunshot wounds attended to. Adam consented and turned to Cassidy.

"You better come with us. We should report Matts to the police."

"Matts! Police!" Mikayla cried. "What on earth did that man do this time?" Her eyes grew large and full of fear, as she suspected Matts was the one who previously shot Adam.

Cassidy quickly told the story of Matts stealing their map, then trying to shoot them to hide evidence of his involvement. She described how Adam fought with Matts and managed to knock the gun temporarily away from him, then wrestle Matts over the cliff, and how Matts landed where the gun had fallen and regained possession of the weapon. Finally, she told how Adam fell into a sink hole. She followed, and Matts waited above to shoot them should they try to get out before the tide filled the basin and drowned them.

It was a horrifying tale as Cassidy went on to explain how they tried desperately to keep afloat until the basin was almost full, breathing the last available air before chancing to swim out, and finally using the force of waves to help carry them to a cliff shelf in order to escape the rising tide. The story was unbelievable, and Adam's mother hugged them both over and over for surviving it.

Mikayla clutched the pirate's coin on the necklace about her throat. When Cassidy finished relating their frightful experience, Mikayla slipped the coin necklace over her head and lay it on the table. "I don't think I want to wear it anymore. That coin has almost cost five lives; Simco, Cassidy, Adam, Mikkel and myself. It also cost my family five years of agony. I wish Raglan Leslie had never given it to me."

Daniel Neilsson picked up the coin necklace, and handed it back to her. "It all depends on how you want to look at it, Mikayla. This pirate's coin gave an old man a dream of adventure until the day he died. It gave Simco a family. It brought Cassidy and Adam, and you and me together as friends, and it brought Mikkel into the world...so I like to think that instead of almost costing five lives, it gifted us with a great big family."

Mikayla retrieved the necklace from Daniel's fingers and slipped it back over her head. "I suppose it depends on how you look at it. I'll give the coin another chance, but it better bring good luck to all of us from now on."

The hospital loaned Adam a set of crutches, so he could walk without putting weight on his leg. He stood resting his weight on the crutches, as Daniel explained to all at his residence, that the x-rays showed Adam had suffered bruising, but no broken bones. However, he did discover two splinters in Adam's knee from his previous hockey injury, and suggested Adam have them removed.

Daniel then turned to the rest of the family. "Adam has suffered a mild concussion, so I want to see him taking it easy for a while. No treasure hunting. Captain Skully's treasure has been hidden for centuries. It can wait a little longer to be discovered. As for his bullet wounds, they are healing well, despite soaking in sea water for half a day."

When Dr. Neilsson was finished giving his diagnosis, Cassidy reported to everyone that she had notified the police about Matts attempted murder plot. The police suggested she and Adam stay hidden at Dr. Neilsson's until they apprehended Matts. The police hoped Matts would feel free to appear in public, as he assumed Cassidy and Adam were dead.

"I have to return to my shift at work," Daniel informed the family. "So Cassidy, I'm putting you in charge of keeping this man quiet. No doing anything more exciting than wading in the duck pond."

Cassidy and Adam both burst into spontaneous laughter. None of the others guessed that the last time Cassidy and Adam went wading along the shores of the duck pond, they had wound up embracing much too closely, and kissing much too passionately. Cassidy hastened to make a false explanation for her and Adam's sudden burst of amusement at not doing anything exciting at the duck pond. "We found…the ducks…amusing."

The others stared at her in silence. "The ducks were…chasing a water beetle." The frail excuse raised quite a few eyebrows, especially Mikayla's. Adam tried unsuccessfully to suppress a grin, and lowered his head to avoid any sign of guilt.

"Keep your secrets," Mikayla burst out to rescue Cassidy, whose cheeks had flushed bright pink in embarrassment. "Time to get supper ready." The women hurried off to the kitchen while Adam's father took Mikkel out to play. That left Adam and Cassidy alone in the living room.

Adam rested on his crutches and shook his head. "The ducks were…chasing a water beetle? A water beetle? …You couldn't come up with a better explanation than that?"

Cassidy put her hands on her hips in frustration. "Well, I didn't hear you offer any help."

Adam continued to laugh at her ridiculous explanation. "I guess it was better than telling the truth…that my kiss knocked your socks off."

Cassidy rolled her eyes at his arrogance. "Don't be a smarty pants. I could knock both your socks off with one good kick at those crutches."

"You wouldn't dare," he warned back.

The moment the comment slipped from his lips, Adam was sorry, for Cassidy's leg whipped like a boomerang under one of his crutches and sent him flying backwards onto the sofa. Adam was not to be defeated so easily, and hooked one crutch around her leg, dragging her forward on top of him.

Mikayla happened into the room and said, "Oops sorry."

"It's not what it looks like," Adam explained hastily. "She attacked me. I was fighting her off."

"You liar," Cassidy exploded, as she struggled off of his body.

"You deliberately knocked my legs out from beneath me. Admit it," Adam accused with a smirk on his lips.

Mikayla threw her arms up in the air. "Adam, do I have to make you eat dirt again?"

Adam's mouth dropped open in shock. "You women always stick together." He limped off to the kitchen to find a safer haven in numbers.

Mikayla observed an embarrassed Cassidy straightening her blouse. "He likes you. Don't hurt him." Then she hustled back to the kitchen to chide her brother, just for the fun of having a brother to pick on.

After a few days of rehabilitation for Adam, the police arrived to inform the couple that Matts had been apprehended. It appeared that Matts visited the local pub to celebrate his belief in destroying any evidence of foul play. The more he drank, the more he bragged about having Captain Skully's treasure map. Finally, someone called him a liar. Matts instantly pulled the map from his pocket and lay it on the bar table as proof of his tales. In excitement to study the map, one drinking buddy spilled a mug of beer over the map. The map was a mere computer printout, so the ink smeared and rendered the map unreadable. Furious, Matts broke a bottle over the man's head, a fight broke out, police were called and that was the end of Matt's treasure hunting.

With threats now eliminated, Adam's parents made flight plans to return back home to Salter River. Adam and Cassidy did likewise, while Dr. Neilsson invited Mikayla and Mikkel to stay at his residence until legal matters could be settled with her divorce and full custody of Mikkel.

Adam's injured leg improved, and early in the morning on the day they were to leave for Canada, he walked down to the duck pond without crutches. Cassidy could see him standing on the embankment, looking out across the waters. She left her partially packed suitcase and walked down the embankment to join him.

"Are you watching the ducks chase water beetles?" she asked from behind him, and he turned and smiled at their mutual joke.

They were silent for a while. Adam finally strolled over to a large willow whose trunk divided and spread to create a horizontal seat wide enough for several to sit upon. Cassidy followed and sat beside him. Adam waited to see if she would mention her words of love for him that she had spoken in the water-filled sink-hole. He was disappointed that she had not acknowledged it since their escape to freedom. He interpreted her silence as viewing him simply as a good friend, nothing more, and that her words of love in a life threatening situation were not the sudden revelation he had hoped for.

Finally, Cassidy broke the silence. "Have you ever wanted something so much that it consumes every minute of your day and night?"

Adam answered quietly, "Don't worry. Skully's treasure will be out there waiting for you when you come back."

Cassidy rose from where she was sitting and faced him. She stepped in close and feathered both her hands through his wild black hair. "I wasn't talking about the treasure. I was talking about you."

Adam looked at her as if not quite believing what he was hearing. As she slowly moved in closer, he half expected Cassidy to turn and run away again, but instead, she lowered her lips on his, and Adam was drawn into a wave he could not escape from.

Adam whispered, "Oh, Cass. I can't imagine my life without you anymore. Marry me."

"I'd marry you this moment," Cassidy replied, her hands caressing his face tenderly, "but I want my Mom and Dad at my wedding, and my aunt and cousins, a couple close friends, your relatives and friends…oh, and Simco…and Waldo, of course."

Adam laughed. "Yes, Waldo, of course…and I'm Italian. Need I say more? Momma would die of heartbreak if I got married without using the guest list she has compiled for the last forty years, while waiting for me to get married."

Cassidy laughed until tears of joy dampened her eyes. "Then what are we waiting for?" She eagerly pulled Adam to his feet. "Let's tour Gotland Island today as our engagement trip."

Adam hugged her to his chest. "We still have our motorcycle. We could enjoy many of the island's historical places before we leave for Canada. Then surprise the family at the airport tonight with an engagement ring on your finger. "

The couple packed their backpacks like a pair of eager children preparing for a camping trip. They left their larger suitcases for Adam's parents to take to the airport, and hopped on the battered old motorcycle. "We're off to give one more chance at finding the treasure," Cassidy yelled back. "We'll meet you at the airport."

Mikayla waved back with a quiet knowing smile. Perhaps the young couple had already found their treasure. They had found each other.

# 24

Cassidy and Adam spent the rest of the morning journeying around the capital city of Visby. Mikayla had given Cassidy a camera before they left, and now they delighted in taking photographs of themselves at the fascinating fortress wall, and amongst the other historical places from medieval times. Cassidy knew her Mom would enjoy the photographs, and thus, feel a part of their adventure.

In their travels, they stopped at a jewelry shop and had the jeweler insert a small, blue sapphire stone into a setting with a larger center diamond. "The blue stone represents my first engagement ring from him," she explained. The jeweler gave her a weird glance, so she added, "It's a long story. The first one belonged to his sister."

The jeweler said nothing, but when they left, he shook his head and muttered, "Canadians!"

The couple biked to the top of the cliffs, and watched a swirl of foam curl around the shore rocks in S formations. "I am sure the treasure is somewhere along here," Mikayla stated. "We just have to figure out the connection between the three rauk fossils to the S formations of foam around these rocks."

"His map showed three sword-like fossils, one on top of another on the rauk," Adam deliberated, looking down on the sea from his perch on the rocky table top. "The clues must have something to do with the number three. Three what? Three kilometers…three ships…

Cassidy stood up to have a better view of the coast line. "It's full tide now, and all I can see in that cove over there is the top of three rocks. The tide comes in approximately every twelve hours. Unfortunately, we have no time today to come back when the tide is down. Let's pick up a lunch and eat in our little farmhouse in the valley, just for old times' sake."

"Before we do, we should visit the owner of the property, tell him our story, and ask permission to use the old cottage. Our other visits were emergencies, but now I feel like we would be trespassing."

Cassidy nodded her head in agreement and they hopped on their motorcycle to hunt for the owner of the vacant farm.

Visiting the owner of the abandoned old farm house proved to be very beneficial to Cassidy and Adam in searching for the treasure. The elderly woman listened intently to their tale, her steel blue eyes brightening at the mention of Ulf Lindberg, who was well known to the islanders as a criminal.

"Do you think there is any truth to the story of Skully's treasure and his runic sword?" Cassidy asked, thinking that if there was such a character as Captain Skuli Hanns, the elderly woman would surely have heard of him.

"Pirate tales are as numerous as the ancient coins found on Gotland," she smiled, her face wrinkled by time and sun. "Some stories are true. Some are not, and some are grains of sand; little dribbles of the truth."

The woman pulled herself to her feet with the aid of her cane and limped off into a bedroom. She returned with a faded sketch of a dagger with runic inscriptions on the blade. "My grandfather gave me this sketch when I was a child. I would sit at his feet and beg for pirate stories. He believed the dagger was from our forefathers, and thought the runic inscription read, "Pass Not". My grandfather insisted he was related to Captain Skully. Said the nasty pirate plundered down the coast, and took anything in his path, including women. Told me stories about him treasuring this runic dagger from his ancestors, thinking the weapon had protective powers."

The woman eyed them closely for a moment, as if deciding on whether to trust the young couple or not. "Now, I trust to lend this drawing to you, so you can copy it, and return it to me. I don't know if it will help you with your search, but you might find a connection somewhere…and don't worry about me laying any claim to Skully's loot. Likely the story about me being related to the scoundrel is as crazy as the story about Skully having a compulsive condition that caused him to want everything in threes. People often add tidbits to a story to make it more interesting, so that may not be true. However, my grandfather insisted Captain Skully did everything in threes, and always chose the left of three things first."

The knowledge about Skully's compulsiveness for the number three opened new doors in Cassidy and Adam's search for his treasure. That afternoon, as they ate their lunch in the old farmhouse, Cassidy and Adam's minds burst alive with fresh ideas.

"Let's start at the beginning," Adam suggested. "The rauk shows three dagger-like fossils, one on top of the other, which matches up with the three daggers at the beginning on the map. Would he consider the bottom one as first, or the top one as first? And what are the three daggers trying to tell us?"

Cassidy shook her head in equal confusion. "I also wonder about those three rock-tops above the tide in the cove. If looking from his ship at sea, the one to the left would be first on the northern side. But if he was standing on shore, the first one to the left would be on the southern side."

Cassidy began packing up their left-over meal. She stacked dishes one on top of each other and then stopped. "That's it!" she exclaimed in excitement. "He buried his treasures one on top of the other. He would bury the runic treasure first, and then another treasure on top so if the first was discovered, they would never think to dig deeper for the other." She clapped her hands in excitement at her revelation. "He copied the stacked fossils."

"If it was me" Cassidy continued, "I would bury my most precious treasure first and make sure it was concealed well under rocks and soil. Then I would bury a less valuable treasure on top. I would want people to discover the upper treasure, as that would insure no one would return to search further. I would bait the treasure…maybe sprinkle a handful of coins and a few jewels on the surface of the ground to encourage people to dig up the top treasure in that location. The sprinkled coins on top would be considered as the third treasure. Over centuries, some of the

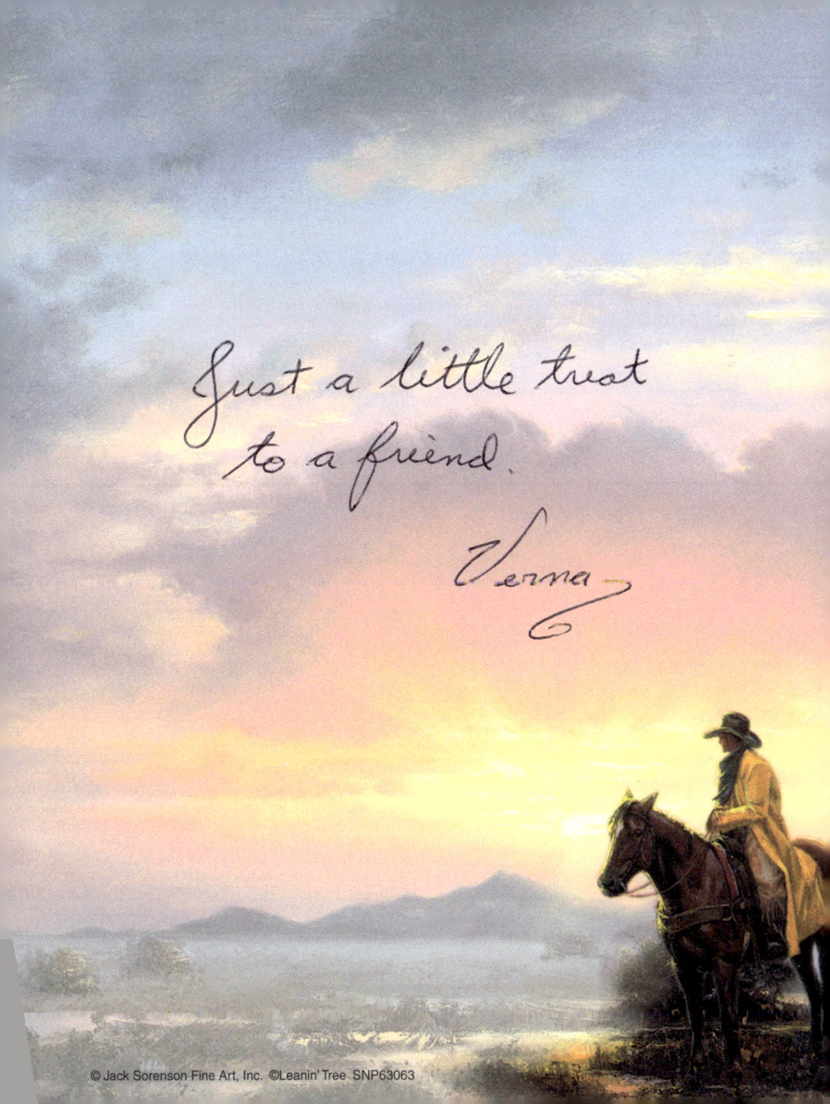
Just a little treat
to a friend.
Verna

coins might have eventually washed down to the shores of the Baltic Sea where Uncle Raglan's wife discovered one. I know that seems a bit stretched for a story, but it could have happened."

"It makes more sense than anything else we've come up with," Adam agreed. "We may never know exactly what Captain Skully did, but I think you are right about burying his treasure in layers. That really matches up with the dagger-like fossils on the rauk."

"I don't think we have time to search for the treasure much longer," Cassidy said sadly. "It's afternoon and we must get ready for the airport in a few hours. We will have to return to the island another time to continue our search." Cassidy wrapped her arms around Adam's neck. "No one knows our secret about Skully, so our exploration will be safe until we return. It will make for an interesting honeymoon."

# 25

Everyone was much pleased, but not surprised, at the beautiful engagement ring on Cassidy's finger at the airport. Leaving Mikayla and Mikkel on the island with the doctor was not easy for the Lucino family to do after recently being reunited, but the happiness and relief of having any threat from Ulf Lindberg eliminated, kept all in good spirits as they boarded the plane.

Cassidy returned to work as a dentist. Adam returned to work as apartment manager and grounds keeper. Simco was delighted with Cassidy and Adam's plans to revitalize the Salter River Mansion into a dance studio, and residence for themselves with Simco employed as head security. Mikayla's divorce from Ulf was almost final, and her full custody of Mikkel granted. Two weddings were now in the future with Daniel and Mikayla also becoming engaged.

Ulf Lindberg and Matts received lengthy sentences for the attempted murders on Simco and Adam, while Henrik received a smaller sentence for his lesser involvement. As for Lars, he had completely disappeared off the face of the earth with twenty million dollars in cash.

The search for Skully's pirate treasure had not been forgotten, as Cassidy and Adam anxiously awaited their honeymoon on Gotland Island in September, where they planned to continue their treasure hunting. They decided to spend the summer compiling a list of where all known treasures had been discovered, and if any were near where they suspected Skully's treasure to be, then they would hopefully, proceed to dig deeper in those locations, anticipating the treasure to be buried beneath where another had been discovered.

They realized that since medieval times, many treasures would have been discovered or retrieved by the pirates themselves. Still, they felt encouraged in their knowledge that Captain Skully had a compulsion for groupings of three, and this condition may have caused the pirate to bury his treasures one on top of the other like the fossils on the rauk.

One July afternoon, a parcel arrived at Adam's residence. He turned it over several times, frowning at the address to "My Big Buddy" in care of Adam Lucino. The moment he opened the parcel, he phoned Cassidy at work and told her to come over immediately, and bring the police.

When Cassidy and the police arrived, they found a puzzled Adam sitting at his table with one million dollars in Canadian currency piled in front of him. He looked as if he had just won the lottery. "It was mailed to me from Peru," Adam explained. "...Well, actually it was mailed to Waldo, I think, as it was addressed to "My Big Buddy" in care of me. I think it came from Ulf Lindberg's man, Lars. I have a feeling he kidnapped Waldo to get the chip from his collar, and then decided to split with the cash instead. Seems like Waldo made a friend in the process."

The police retrieved the money to see if it could be traced to any theft or crime, but the money showed up clean. Ulf had successfully managed to launder the money through his sources before he visited Simco, so no trace of the money being illegal was found. The million was therefore, returned to Waldo.

Adam and Cassidy deposited the money in a special account in the bank and then deliberated on what to do with it. "I hate to spend money that was achieved illegally," Adam sighed, "In a way, it's not ours. What would Waldo suggest we do with it?"

Cassidy didn't have to think very long. "I propose you rename your Recreation Centre, "Waldo's Dig" or "Den" or something like that, and spend some of the money adding needed facilities and an outdoor hockey rink to the place. Then lots of kids will benefit from the money. Perhaps if Lars had known a place like yours when he was a youth, he might not have wound up involved with criminals like Ulf."

Adam nodded in agreement, pleased at her suggestion.

Cassidy added, "I also suggest giving Simco a sum. He was shot, and remained hidden for years, working with my uncle to save Mikayla and Mikkel. He deserves a reward for that."

"I don't think Simco will take a dime," Adam said. "He wouldn't even take a tip from Mikayla when he was a taxi driver. But I could likely talk him into giving money in his name to a young baseball team. Mikayla told me he used to cheer for some local baseball team every weekend. Said they couldn't afford uniforms, but could sure play ball. Let's buy the team uniforms and print Simco on them. I think Simco would take a kick out of that."

"I think Waldo is going to have a lot of fun doing good deeds with Lars' gift," Cassidy laughed. "At least, something positive will come out of Lars sense of humor in sending it to a dog. Maybe we should buy Waldo one big steak, just to say thanks for sharing his million."

Adam patted Waldo on the head. "Sounds like a plan. There's a meat market just down the street." Waldo jumped into the back seat of the jeep before Cassidy and Adam could get in the vehicle. There was something in Adam's voice that Waldo interpreted as, "Going for food."

Cassidy laughed at the hound's response to her suggestion, and warned Waldo, "This is a one-time steak, fella. Don't think just because you're a millionaire, that steak is on your menu every day. Even millionaires need to budget." Waldo barked, as if he understood the deal.

Then Cassidy's thoughts deepened. She looked down and twirled the beautiful engagement ring on her finger, signifying an engagement that she could not have imagined happening such a short time ago. "Strange, how a simple pirate coin found by Uncle Raglan's wife on the beach of Gotland Island so many years ago, could cause all of this to happen. It seems unreal."

"Yes," Adam agreed. "You will have to write a book about it someday." Adam put his hand in his pocket to withdraw his wallet for buying Waldo a steak. He discovered a handmade valentine in his pocket. "What's this?"

"My heart!" Cassidy laughed. "I'll explain it to you someday...I wonder what I could put as an ending to the story?"

Adam leaned over and kissed her lips tenderly. "Just say the gardener won the princess's heart and that their adventures have just begun...because somewhere on Gotland Island, a pirate's treasure has slept for a thousand years, and is waiting for them."

*Eleven Years later:*

Adam, Daniel and fifteen year old Mikkel Neilsson took turns digging in the rocky soil of the cave. The atmosphere was intense with anticipation. A family group consisting of Cassidy, Mikayla, ten year old Carter Lucino, his eight year old sister, Jasper, and ten year old twin cousins, Hanna and Heather Neilsson stood at the top of the deep hole, and waited for the sound of the mens' shovels to hit a chest buried a thousand years before. The four young children yelled down to their brother and fathers in excitement, "Have you hit China yet? - "Are there some rings and pearls for us?" - "Is the pirate sword on top of the treasure?" - "Will the chest be heavy?"

Even Alaska, Waldo's pup, barked down the hole as if asking the treasure hunters if a couple dog bones might possibly be buried along with the pirate loot for him and his father.

Mikkel called up to his sisters and cousins. "Not there quite yet, but..." His shovel clunked on something solid in the soil. He knelt down and carefully brushed soil and dust away from the top of a chest. Adam and Daniel cleared more soil from around the chest and then hoisted it up to the surface, where Cassidy and Mikayla grabbed hold of the handles, and dragged it to the surface. The men climbed out of the hole and stood in a circle about the chest, hearts beating wildly.

"People have been searching for this treasure for a thousand years," Cassidy said with quiet reflection. "It feels strange that I should be the one to open the chest after all this time." She beckoned Mikayla to join her.

The women looked at each other, then smiled at their husbands who had helped them search for the treasure for the past eleven years. Carter and Mikkel rushed to unbuckle the straps around the chest, so their mothers could open the chest. Then Cassidy and Mikayla knelt together beside the chest and gingerly opened the lid, as if expecting Captain Skully to jump out like a genie in a lamp.

It was as if a light bulb had been turned on inside. A luminous pile of silver and gold coins mingled with jeweled bracelets, strings of cultured pearls, and other valuable pirate booty...but no runic dagger."

Cassidy glanced up at Adam. "Do you honestly think Captain Skully would have the nerve to bury ALL his treasures in layers?"

Adam started to laugh at the thought, and at the reaction of the others. The girls were joyously stringing pearls about their necks and slipping over-sized rings upon their fingers. The boys were intently studying the country origin on the coins, while Daniel and Mikayla were comparing the pecking marks on her coin necklace to the ones in the chest. All were having the time of their lives.

"I wouldn't put it past the devil," Adam chuckled to Cassidy. "Looks like this isn't the Harja file. Somewhere on Gotland Island, a runic dagger is still guarding Skully's last treasure."

Jasper pulled her father's head down and plunked a ruby studded crown upon it. She slipped an ancient engraved bracelet onto her mother's wrist, and then ran off to help decorate Hanna, Heather and Alaska.

"That's fine with me," Cassidy laughed, as she rubbed the gold and jeweled bracelet to a high sheen. She glanced up at Adam, whose newly acquired crown tilted askew on his head. "Are you ready for another adventure…my prince?"

# THE END

Verna Laraine Hutlet (nee Elliott) has entertained many with her writings and paintings since childhood. Many of her writings have been published and has been a Featured Artist at the International Peace Gardens. Verna has been a farm wife, Chief Telephone Supervisor, and a Field Recording Technician for Dairies. She also enjoys photography, music, horses, gardening, sports and country life. Her favorite times are spent with her husband, Robert (Herby), their six children & families. She writes for them and her siblings, and for all those who enjoy her stories.

*Verna's calico eyes (one green, one brown) mirror a mosaic world that she loves to paint and write about.*

## For more adventures please visit:

## vernaelliotthutlet.com

55886156R00123

Made in the USA
Charleston, SC
10 May 2016